As she crept to ___ ___, she could see the corral. S___ ___ously cocking her Colt and stepping forward, Jessie spun around, stopping Kyle the shift boss in mid-lunge, her revolver leveled at his forehead.

"That's my bay, and I'm taking him outta here," she said.

A door she hadn't noticed flew open and knocked her off her feet as she triggered the Colt. Before she knew it, she was being whisked to her feet by the powerful Ryde Benton and dragged helplessly into the stable building. Bringing her into an open shoeing area, Benton knocked her down again with an open hand that felt like a club.

"Feisty little mare, ain't she!" Kyle exclaimed.

"Break her, Ryde, break her!" cried another man.

Benton roared, "I'll break you all right!" and tore open her shirt, sending buttons flying . . .

DON'T MISS THESE
ALL-ACTION WESTERN SERIES
FROM THE BERKLEY PUBLISHING GROUP

THE GUNSMITH by J. R. Roberts
Clint Adams was a legend among lawmen, outlaws, and ladies. They called him . . . the Gunsmith.

LONGARM by Tabor Evans
The popular long-running series about U.S. Deputy Marshal Long—his life, his loves, his fight for justice.

LONE STAR by Wesley Ellis
The blazing adventures of Jessica Starbuck and the martial arts master, Ki. Over eight million copies in print.

SLOCUM by Jake Logan
Today's longest-running action Western. John Slocum rides a deadly trail of hot blood and cold steel.

— WESLEY ELLIS —

LONE STAR

AND THE
REDEMPTION MASSACRE

JOVE BOOKS, NEW YORK

LONE STAR AND THE REDEMPTION MASSACRE

A Jove Book / published by arrangement with
the author

PRINTING HISTORY
Jove edition / January 1994

ISBN: 0-515-11284-4

A JOVE BOOK®
Jove Books are published by The Berkley Publishing Group,
200 Madison Avenue, New York, New York 10016.
JOVE and the "J" design are trademarks belonging to Jove Publications, Inc

PRINTED IN THE UNITED STATES OF AMERICA

10 9 8 7 6 5 4 3 2 1

LONE STAR

AND THE
REDEMPTION MASSACRE

★

Chapter 1

Blood dripped into no ordinary man's eyes the way it did into Orrum Jessup's. The chiseled ridge of his brow and a deep horizontal wrinkle below his left eye drew his blood into two rivulets that intersected like a garnet crucifix. The pistol-whipping they'd given him had put his lamp right out—he didn't know how long—and raised a purple hillock on his head that burned like the near side of hell.

As he came to, shaking loose the fog, the voices became recognizable. The shadowy figures took on familiar faces. He remembered where he was. The small furnace kept the room almost unbearably hot. The dust of mineral ore that smothered everything—the floorboards, the flasks and balancing scales, the shelves lined with bottles and tins, the mortar and pestle, the furnace irons, and especially the spatters of blood on his boots—told him he was still in his assay office. Where Ryde Benton had found him.

Desolate, fallen livid, Orrum retched across the arm of his chair with the sickening realization of what was about to take place. In the chair before him, practically reclining, was Benton, turning away in disgust and cursing beneath his breath. On his enormous lap, beneath his massive fist, lay the Colt he had belted Jessup with. A piece of torn skin still clung to the grip. When Benton turned back, Jessup saw the eyes that were talked about all the way to Sand Creek. All the way back to '64, when the "fighting parson" Chivington had hacked over a hundred Cheyenne out of existence with the help of a large, loyal, ponytailed nineteen-year-old with eerie colorless eyes—named Ryde Benton. The queasy tremble in Jessup's gut fluttered again. Though Benton wore a ten-dollar hat on a five-cent head, he had a cunning glee for venom.

Jessup's very next thought was of his daughter, which only intensified his helplessness, walled him in guilt. For years he had dragged young Arvilla from lonely wilderness to sin-ridden mining camps, exposing her to every discomfort and danger every young girl should rightfully be spared. Remarkably, the experience had sharpened rather than dulled her. It lit an ember of feistiness in her that intensified as she matured. Became defiance. Hardheadedness—her most valuable quality, he figured. That girl's got eight acres o'hell in her, he thought, and thank goodness she can read. If it hadn't been for some good hearts . . . But there on the table lay the yellow paper these thugs wanted him to sign. In his mouth clung the taste of his own blood, the grit of broken teeth, and wringing his heart like the neck of a hen, guilt, for Jessup knew he'd soon be leaving Arvilla utterly alone in the world.

Benton's low, airy voice sounded like it came from the mouth of a cavern. "Sooner you sign that there paper, sooner we can all return to the ladies." He thrust a thumb up a nostril and set to yanking on something dry. He didn't blink, though one eye teared when his yanking paid off. "Course you'll have to tell us something about the Talisman before we leave you. Sign the paper. Then we'll talk."

Jessup had no intention to resist signing if it meant he had a chance to come away with his hide. He could tolerate duress. But they had roused him from a deep sleep in the small hours, then bashed him so suddenly after the Decatur

2

kid produced the paper that it took Jessup some time to understand what it was they wanted. His eyes focused with difficulty. He made the paper out to be an assay report—one of his own forms—and it had some numbers filled in, not in his hand. Certainly not the numbers he would have recorded for ore samples from the Gore mill. Benton wanted him to falsify some gram weights of ore and silver. No surprise there. Nor was it surprising that Benton hadn't given a thought to all the other numbers recorded in Jessup's notebooks that would betray the lie—mass of fluxes, cupel sizes, bead mass . . . Counterfeiting didn't have to be elegant in these parts of Colorado. Benton fit right in. Jessup pulled himself up to reach a pen. His right hand—the one missing a finger—shook badly as he aimed for the inkwell. As Jessup scratched his name across the page, Benton rested one foot on the arm of Jessup's chair and spoke in a breathy whisper.

"Now. Talisman, Orrum. Tell me about the Talisman."

Jessup's eyes were open but not seeing anything. His hesitation resulted in Benton's heavy-heeled boot slamming him across the side of his face.

"Where is it?" he growled.

Badly shaken, his voice trembling, Jessup said, "I signed your assay. Alls it needs is my stamp and it's good as gold. Awright? I can't noways talk about the Talisman, I—"

With another swift kick to Jessup's head that glanced off his shoulder, Benton spat through his teeth, "Tell me, you piece of shit! I ain't got all night." He planted his feet on the floor and closed in. "We know the outcrop is on Atwood's land. How close to the property line? Which way does it drift?"

There'd be a Fourth of July parade in Hell before Jessup would tell Benton the location of the Talisman lode. It was Jessup's own discovery after more than twelve years of mucking, lumbering, and risking his life underground. For years before and since learning the assayer's science, he had stubbornly prospected the hills north of Bear River when everyone else had given up and packed out for the San Juans. He had scoured the Gore Range below Lynx Pass when not tied up with assays, betting against logic that there was still a mother lode waiting to be found. It was apparent the northern finds were beginning to pay out. Benton's presence now was proof of that. In fact, Jessup's partner, the Honorable Jefferson Davis Atwood, a once-respected circuit judge for Rio Blanco County and founding owner of Grand River Mining, had sold off a hefty parcel just north of the Flattops on Jessup's word alone. Sold it to none other than Benton's boss, Charles Calvin Padgett, president of the Gore Mining and Milling Company, the region's largest and oldest operation of its kind. There had been no deception on Atwood's or Jessup's part about the sale. But evidently Padgett suspected the existence of undiscovered treasure; more likely, his thugs merely spied very closely on Jessup's lone excursions along the old Ute trails atop the mesa.

So there it was: Benton wanted information about the Talisman, and Jessup was sworn not to give it, fully aware that his life was therefore worth less than lead and equally aware that revealing his secret would make it worth even less. It was this awareness and his stubborn refusal to cooperate that made Orrum Jessup no ordinary man.

"I signed it," Jessup said quietly as he placed the pen down. "Alls you need is my stamp, and it'll be done official."

Benton sighed as he glanced up at the three impatient men standing in the heat. He asked what stamp Jessup was talking about as he holstered the Colt, and the assayer slid a weighty contraption toward himself. Benton watched as Jessup slipped the paper beneath the circular platen and, leaning down on the curved handle, embossed his official seal onto the report. Inspecting the neat impression, Benton marveled. "Hmm, ain't that something? I just wonder what else this here thing can do."

Taking his cue, a thick-armed, foul-smelling mucker stepped behind Jessup and surprised him with a headlock as

Benton's vice-like hand clamped down on his wrist. Swiftly, Benton had one of Jessup's fingers caught under the platen of the embosser and leaned on the handle. Jessup's cry was stilted by a bottomless feeling in the pit of his stomach that almost made him faint. Momentarily the pain in his head was forgotten, replaced by nausea at the crackling sound of bone yielding beneath metal. Through watering eyes, Jessup's glance was met by Ryde Benton's seemingly jovial eyes and what Jessup could only guess was a smile.

"I think you best tell me something about the Talisman. Or maybe you really want to lose another finger? Is that it?" He chuckled, adding, "Hey, at least people will know who this one belongs to, with that official-like seal on there." He stole a snickering glance at his cohorts.

"I do expect that's truth, Ryde," laughed the Decatur kid. The fourth man, who was inspecting shelves along the back wall, turned to watch. He wore a red neckerchief.

Benton said, "Now I 'ppreciate you signing this here assay, Jessup, but, honest injun, it ain't worth a rat's ass to me. What's important to me is the Talisman." He reconsidered a moment, then, sitting on the table while keeping his hand on the embosser, he continued, "Let me put it this way, Jess. Look at your cutoff finger." He laughed, "Hell! How you gonna look at the gol'dang thing? *It ain't there!*"

The neckerchief, playing with glass bottles, snorted.

"Evidently it's long gone, and everybody knows how you got it took from you. Am I right?" His boys mumbled their affirmation. "You was being robbed, and you was too fence-post stubborn to give up a little ol' wedding ring that weren't no good anyways. Hell, boy, you can't be married to a long-gone slut! Am I right?

"Now this Talisman lode you found. Chances are right good that there lode lies most on Padgett's land. Think about it. You found the spot what shows aboveground, is all. See? Now if Atwood and you was fixin' to go diggin' up what ain't yours rightful-like, that would be the same

5

as chopping off Padgett's own finger for his gold, now wouldn't it?"

"Damn right," slurred the Decatur kid. The fourth man coughed after uncorking a flask and taking a whiff. Jessup recognized the red bandanna. It marked the man as one of the Blossom Rock Guards. Padgett's own private militia.

Leaning close to Jessup's face, Benton repeated, "Wouldn't it?" and added pressure on the embosser.

With effort, Jessup defiantly squealed, "No."

Keeping his grip on the handle, Benton backhanded Jessup with the other fist, then hauled the metal embosser side-arm to arc into Jessup's skull, whereupon Benton fell on him, flailing fists the mass of mallets, sending the embosser rumbling to the floorboards and throwing Jessup over in his chair. A wooden knock was Jessup's head making impact. Decatur and the other two stayed back, and after many thunderous poundings, Benton's fury subsided. He stood erect. Straightened his vest. He kicked Jessup square in the gut as the man lay helpless in the dust, one finger standing oddly straight, unable to close within his four-fingered fist.

Benton restrained himself from another lunge. He couldn't kill Jessup yet. The idea threw him into a dither to devise some clever suffering for the assayer, something memorable and right this moment. Something that would fire Benton's own mind. He scanned the cabin. "Here!" cried the one who had coughed. He snatched a labeled flask off the shelf and held it out. Benton couldn't see the label.

"What?"

"You know I can't read, Ryde, but it sure do sting some."

Benton grabbed the flask. "Nit-Ric . . . Ni-Tric. Nitric acid. Get'm up here!"

The cabin vibrated under their boot heels as they righted Jessup in the chair and slid him beneath the swaying kerosene lamp. The Decatur kid turned away upon seeing his eye bleeding.

6

"Take off his shirt," said Benton.

When Benton uncorked the flask, Jessup convulsed upward with a hollow "Nooo!" and swung his good hand to knock away the flask, but missed it. Benton held it aside, and Jessup tore at the big man's shirt, ripped it open, and scratched his chest. A beefy fist to Jessup's jaw jarred his skull, the ultimate blow his previous beating had spared him. His eyes dimmed.

Stepping back, Benton gathered himself, set down the flask. On his bare chest, a small rectangular pouch made of canvas hung by a cord from his neck. He stuffed it into his shirt before noticing his buttons had popped off. He wiped sweat from his eyes and lip. Adjusted his shirtsleeve. "Stretch him over the table." Picked up the flask and carefully set the cork loosely in the top. "Get his shirt off."

The one who stunk—he stunk like a mule's ass on a summer's day—ran a blade through the back of Jessup's collar and tore the shirt down the middle to his waist. He cut a swath and gagged him, twisting the two ends around one hand. One man on each wrist, they leaned Jessup over the table, his torso locked between the chair and the table's edge. Benton squatted to see Jessup at eye level. His thighs were thick like a stallion's, and his fingernails hoarded age-old dirt. One fist held the vaporous flask within Jessup's sight. Strands of Benton's wiry black hair, loosened from his ponytail, caught the light like a perverse halo.

"It's so simple," Benton cajoled, and Jessup knew it was true. There was Benton, there the flask. They had the knives, guns, and muscle. Jessup had the secret—and the life to lose. "Anybody could see how simple this is. An imbecile," Benton said, "a absolute friggin' pea-brained imbecile could see. You're going to talk about Talisman now."

Benton rose with a sigh. One of the boys whooped quietly to himself, and another swore through his teeth in anticipation of something they had never seen before.

7

Something told Jessup that Benton was tipping the flask. He squeezed his eyes shut, forcing out a tight groan and a reluctant fart, when suddenly near the base of his spine a splash of cold sprouted fangs that pierced and burned. Before the next drops fell, Jessup's back went taut, springing up like bacon on a griddle. His slow, elongated screech was met with gleeful whoops as the thin acid vapor, like a blooded mountain lion intoxicated by the kill, staggered lazily away. To the boys it looked like burning, it hissed like steam, but smelled like nothing they had known. Benton stopped the flow as the welts grew to several inches. Long moments passed before Jessup's stifled screams died away.

"Now, Orrum," lured Benton, bending down to him, "don't you see? What if the Talisman's outcrop is actually on Gore property? All this will turn out the same either way. You know how these damn claim bound'ries are always being disputed."

One of the men snickered, "Yeah—not for long."

"Listen, Orrum. This could save your life."

Jessup knew Benton lied. After all, a killer kills. Ryde Benton: self-proclaimed legend of the Indian wars. "Mine Superintendent"—for lack of anything more believable—who came from white Tennessee trash that couldn't keep a farm. Padgett's right-hand man, hired gun, and source of sick entertainment.

Benton was becoming irked. "Don't be stupid, Orrum." He splashed a few more vicious beads of acid, which elicited an explosive cry from Jessup. "Talisman ain't gonna save you."

Jessup whimpered a prayer and blurted, "I'll tell. Please, God—I'll tell you. 'Bout fifteen, eighteen miles south from your number one concentrating mill, the old one, 'cross the Bear near where Padgett had them Utes cleared out—maybe three hours out. Follow Small Kill Creek toward Flattop. There's a cleared trail along the first saddle on the Dome Creek side. There. You'll see it."

8

The flask came to rest on a counter. From near the bucking board where ore samples were crushed, Benton lifted a pail of water and doused the fires on Jessup's back. He commended him while the boys stood him up, and he quickly reviewed his directions aloud. Pacing the cabin like a prize cock, Benton swaggered past his tortured quarry and gloated. More than once he raised his palms, saying, "Just had to be, Orrum . . . Simple!" He pulled a natty blanket from atop a chest of drawers and gallantly swept it around Jessup's slumped shoulders. The assayer flinched, barely able to see in one eye, but down came the blanket, suffocating in the cabin's heat. And closer came Benton, cooing, "Now that weren't too ugly. That's all there is to it," as he drew from behind him a long knife with a fluted blade of blued steel and swiftly thrust it up inside Jessup's rib cage, hugging him snugly with one arm around the back while jacking the blade to its hilt, then lifted the thin man off the floor, hissing into his contorted face the words of his hero Chivington, "Nits make lice," and twisting his fist until he felt the blade's edge touch bone. With barely a sputter, Benton threw Jessup's crumpled frame to the floor to writhe around the impaling weapon. Finally, after several long minutes, he put one boot to Jessup's chest and slowly pulled out the bone-handled blade—with one last twist, the boys would later swear.

Wiping the knife on Jessup's shirt, Benton bellowed, "Let's get him outta here." He folded the blanket over the dying man to contain the blood and supervised the others in carrying him to the buckboard outside.

Ten minutes later the wagon came to a jerky stop. Jessup was still alive, though barely. He couldn't tell if it was a terribly cold night or if this was what dying felt like. Having no urge to shiver, he figured he knew the answer. None of that mattered to Benton's men. It could have been an ore bag thudding the gate of the wagon when Jessup's head spilled off the back. Too late for them to be thinking about the ladies by now. The cold was starting to bite, and the men wanted to get home.

The breeze carried brief gusts of warm air to them from the gaping mouth, the adit, of a man-made cave looming before them on the hillside. "Keepsake" was burned into a plank nailed to the collar of the mine's portal. Near the summit above towered the shaft house, touching the sky. They stood on a level plot facing a slope stripped of timber. Small-gauge rails curved from the square hole to a small stamp mill perched above a hill of tailings. Two men carried Jessup along the rails. Benton and the other one lit a couple of lanterns and hurried ahead into the blackness.

It was tough going even with the light. The rails were strewn with rubble, or slick with mud, or spiked with splintered boards. Old iron candle holders were still pinned into the stone walls. Picks and shovels and other rusted tools lay in heaps. They walked steadily deeper, the air becoming rank and warm, until the Decatur boy looked back at Benton, who led them into a wide stope elaborately stripped and shored with timber. From there sank a double shaft. On the far side stood a steam-driven hoist for lifting ore; on the near side, an outdated mule-driven hoist—and one sickly mule—for hoisting crewmen.

Beyond, the tunnel forked, one side being the drift that followed the strike deep into the mountain. The other side was the original drift, a low-ceilinged pillar mine nicknamed "Sightless." It had paid out years before, earning its name by being a blind apex, a dead end in the vein. The added danger of being an untimbered mine, with natural rock pillars supporting an entire mountain of overburden, left the Sightless little used and only reluctantly refilled with tailings. Entrance to it was barred by a sawhorse bearing a sign: "DANGER—Do Not Enter."

The hanging wall made it increasingly difficult to carry Jessup, so Benton ordered them to lay him in a small wooden ore car. Had the light in the mine been any better, they would sooner have noticed their hands turning red from

10

the blood-soaked blanket. They did notice how sticky their hands were becoming. When they heaved Jessup higher, a low moan echoed through the tunnel, startling them.

"Put him down awhile," Benton ordered. Holding his lantern high, he stooped to open the blanket.

A red patina covered Jessup's entire body, so much had he bled into the wool. His eyes rolled and he gurgled through pale red bubbles. With Herculean effort, he spoke. "Get you . . . will get you—"

"I'll be damned," said the bad-smelling one. "Sombitch just won't give it up."

Benton pointed. "Hand me that axe, will ya, boy?" Exchanging his lantern for the long-handled tool, he kicked Jessup's right arm outward, across a railway tie. "Don't rightly know what it is your aiming to get, old son, but I reckon to get me a souvenir."

The axe head sparked against the low ceiling at the top of Benton's arcing swing, but he didn't lose momentum in bringing it down upon Jessup's livid wrist, to sever the four-fingered hand and elicit a nervous giggle from the kid. Jessup's simpering cry was one of surrender. Benton ordered him into the ore car.

They threw him in carelessly, and he tumbled into an unnatural, twisted position. Benton meanwhile lifted the cold hand by the middle finger and, tossing it to Decatur, called out, "Hey, kid, *catch*!" when it was already airborne. The kid fumbled with it across his chest and let it fall as he gasped. Although he tried to maintain a manly composure, he was visibly shaken and embarrassed by Benton's snickering.

"Help me," said the murderer to the thick-armed man, and together they pushed the ore car along its rails, hand-tramming deeper into the hellish dark, having to crouch more the farther they went. The car gained speed as the mine sloped downward. From there on, the Sightless was an inclined shaft, with bottomless crosscuts angling down from the footwall to either side of the rails, thick with the

11

stench of sulphur, manure, and rotting garbage.

The man trotting beside Benton left off as the car picked up speed, but Benton stayed with it, pushing it onward, ever faster, until a change in the clattering echo warned him the dead end was near. With a great final thrust, he shoved himself away from the car, watching it rise off its rails as it struck rubble and toppled itself end over end, dumping Jessup's broken figure across a mound of jagged stone and pinning both his legs.

All the boys heard next was Benton's labored breathing, like that of a dragon in its lair, issuing from the void. A nervously quiet moment elapsed, and they itched to leave. Expecting to see Benton emerge from the blackness, they instead heard the sound of splashing water, having no idea it was Benton pissing on Jessup's body until they saw him return to light, buttoning his pants, bending to retrieve his souvenir.

Orrum Jessup died like no ordinary man. He had withstood the brutality for as long as he could and was almost relieved it had ended. As their gravelly footfalls faded toward the portal of the Sightless, Orrum slid his icy hand up his shirt, probing. He managed to touch the locket that hung close to his heart and enfold it in his fingers just as his last, long breath hissed from his collapsing chest. Jessup was stone dead. And Benton and his men stepped into the cold, clean air as the rising sun bloodied itself upon the brooding peaks above this bad side of Purgatory, this violent, mud-caked mining town named Redemption.

★

Chapter 2

Traveling bag in hand, Jessica Starbuck stood before a fire-blackened ruin near the top of narrow, noisy Eagle Road. Once an imposing building, the collapsed walls, melted flues, and brick chimneys now lay piled within the remains of the exterior frame. Just below the brick step at the roadside and spattered with mud lay a charred sign, broken off at one end to read, "Pinnacles Ho."

"Pinnacles Hotel," Jessie muttered. "Wonderful."

Her butt and legs hummed with the dull ache of a long journey. She gazed up and down the fog-hazed street while the smell of fire stabbed her throat. She was oblivious to the succession of men—in wagons, on foot, some haggard, soiled, or bearded, others wearing clean vests and collared shirts—who stared in wonderment at the sight of this comely lass, certainly a lady, with her long, copper-blond tresses tucked beneath the brown Stetson slung down her back on a thong. Above her green tweed skirt, her riding jacket clung enough to broadcast to everyone what a remarkably well-endowed, hourglass figure she had, blessed with sumptuous high breasts, flat stomach, and plush, round derriere.

13

Downhill along the muddy thoroughfare, it seemed the air was stifled with a smoky mist that grayed out the steep, rocky hills rising behind the buildings. No structure was more than two stories high. The road was lined on both sides by the false-front cupboards, many with roofed wooden sidewalks filled with men in dark clothing—only men, it seemed—who seemed heedless of the congestion and odor. The haze had a yellowish tint to it, the foul exhalations of the nearby smelters. Manure and earth came together in a heady scent. Empty bottles and playing cards littered the ruts that slurped beneath the mud-caked wheels of dozens of buckboards. Teamsters navigated around open ditches and logs piled about, on which sat men in crumpled fedoras, turning their heads to gawk at Jessie.

Wooden signs jutted into the street from above doorways or below second-floor windows: "Lodgepole Saloon," "Hardwick & Knowles Jewelry Manufactory," "St. Ives Parlor," "M. Gillis & Son Dry Goods," "The Paydirt," "Livery," "B.D.'s Tonsorial," "Treber Liquor Sales." Every other business seemed to be a saloon. Where the road curved down into the gulch, Jessie noticed smaller cabins nestled together, painted white, with lazy wisps of smoke rising in the still air above them, and the cross of a small church peeking over the rooftops. A large wagon laden with half a dozen coffins trundled around the bend to disappear behind the buildings.

So this is Redemption, she thought. God help us.

"God help you, miss," said a wild-eyed skeleton of a man, as if reading her mind. Wringing the brim of his hat, he passed on, furtively looking over his shoulder. "God bless . . ."

"Excuse me!" she called after him, "Is this— Was this the Pinnacles Hotel?"

" 'Fraid so, ma'am, the Pinnacles. God help 'em . . . for thus sayest the Lord of hosts: I will smelt them and test them."

Great, she thought. Everyone here is crazy, too.

Avoiding several pools of brown water, Jessie slogged her way across the road to the wooden walk and proceeded along the street. Men paused in their tracks to watch her, heads turned, and in front of a seedy lodging house, a singsong voice said, "Hello, pretty!"—a woman's voice, which drew Jessie's reluctant attention. She turned to see a girl younger than herself wearing too much rouge. "Care to relax with me and a drink upstairs?"

In another world—the one in which Jessie had been educated about such things by her father's Japanese housekeeper, a highly honored courtesan at one time—Jessie thought sex was just as simple and free as this young woman did, but not nearly as meaningless. It wasn't confused with evil or filth; it was healthy. Sacred. This poor girl looked decidedly unhealthy. And sad.

Continuing along the walk, Jessie took notice of a more respectable-looking establishment, the Touchstone, advertising on its frosted pane windows, "Lager Beer 10¢ Froth Included"—not cheap, she thought—and "Hot Food Served Good." Outside rested two kegs branded, "Rocky Mt. Brewery, Denver."

Polished brass rails divided the large room lengthwise, drawing Jessie's eyes to the huge caribou head mounted on the rear wall. The bar was coarsely made but handsome. Tacked to the wall behind the mustachioed bartender a sign reading "Pasties 5¢" hung beneath a third-rate painting of a reclining odalisque clothed only in her jewels. Jessie discreetly sized up the place and approached the bar.

The barkeep was respectful enough, but when Jessie asked if he was acquainted with Miss Arvilla Jessup, she couldn't miss the momentary drift of his eyes over her shoulder. His answer was a stammering "Sorry, ma'am, don't believe I've had the pleasure" that rung false. Nonetheless, she explained that she had expected to lodge at the recently destroyed Pinnacles, and could he direct her toward whoever had assumed the hotel's affairs?

15

"Terrible sorry, ma'am. But no one hereabouts knows where they might be since the fire."

Jessie huffed, stealing a glance around the room, feigning confusion. There were only eight other people there, most sitting on the far side of the rail. Two pairs of grubby men sat eating and examining her, undressing her in their minds.

"I'll have a beer, please," she ordered, " . . . with froth."

"One beer . . ."

Slamming the large mug on the oak, the bartender knocked off much of the froth. Upon seeing Jessie's paper money, he frowned darkly and rolled his eyes. Then Jessie noticed a sign: "Gold, Silver, or Scrip, Please. Paper Burns," and another: "In Gold We Trust." She hesitated before reaching for her money, then, opening her jacket wide enough for the bartender to see the butt of the derringer in her pocket, she reached in and withdrew a half eagle. Staring directly into her incredible green eyes, the bartender thanked her and brought her change.

She took a seat at a table with her back to the wall. The lager felt cool slipping into her chest, and after another long draft, she licked the white foam from her lips, only to lock eyes with a hungry-looking miner. She turned away with a sneer.

Her body relaxed for the first time in nearly two weeks, having traveled overland from Fort Sumner, at the head of the trail Chisolm laid out in '75, upon receiving Arvilla's urgent telegram. It seemed a lifetime since she had left home in West Texas, the Circle Star ranch, to meet her buyers at the Fort Sumner cattle terminals.

Although only in her twenties, Jessie had assumed all the responsibilities of her father's vast ranch and his many business holdings, and she performed remarkably well. She had to; there was too much at stake—not just the Starbucks' interests, but the entire nation's. There was a silent war being waged, with Jessie often on the front lines. It was raging long before President Hayes took office, before

16

Jessie was born, even before her father, a Texas tycoon, created the import-export business that eventually became the Starbuck empire. It was a war upon America herself, her political institutions and business establishments, by a lawless, unscrupulous, international cabal intent on taking control. During a series of bloody trade wars, the cabal had been responsible for the death of Jessie's mother when Jessie was only a child and, later, for the assassination of her father. Her heart was often weighted by the burden of such vast holdings, but more so by an ongoing, gnawing need for vengeance upon her beloved parents' murders.

Hers was a vengeance that, unassisted, she would have had little hope of realizing, but her father had seen to many details of her upbringing. He made sure Jessie could handle a gun and a horse as well as social graces and business. He had provided for his daughter well, even to the point of bringing into her life a longtime friend—traveling far from her now—upon whom she could rely as her trusted companion and able bodyguard.

The weight of it all sometimes made her weary to the bone—not the way she would have liked to make the long trip to Redemption. After a hard-sprung coach with horsehair-covered seats to Ft. Lyon, she'd partaken of the relative luxury of "high iron"—the Denver & Rio Grande to the state capital, then the Colorado Central to Georgetown, drawn along by a plucky little Baldwin locomotive. The amazingly engineered railways of Clear Creek Canyon alone made Jessie feel like a true mountain adventurer, rising to giddy heights above the rugged gulch that was the end of the line for the small-gauge rails—and the end of the line for many a miner.

Crossing the range from Georgetown proved an arduous tandem of small coach and muleback. The coach to Silver Plume was really an enclosed buckboard with bench seats and straw padding that felt like no padding at all. The toll road to Eagle was no more than a cliff trail chiseled out of bare mountain rock with hardly a tree to stop the fall

17

of any traveler unlucky enough to be thrown. Jessie was withered by the long, challenging trek, and after a night's rest in Eagle, finally arrived in Marmot Gulch the next morning, marveling at what she saw on the approach to Redemption.

Along every stream and every creek in every gulch were the tents and sluice boxes of miners desperate for El Dorado. Head frames of mines and cockeyed raw pine cabins rose everywhere on the hillsides. Closer to Redemption, the otherwise tranquil alpine wilderness echoed with the clatter and huff of steam-powered hoists and the rumble of avalanches of tailings torn from the mountains' innards. At the mouth of the gulch, the hillsides were shorn of timber and dotted with miners' meager burrows, their projecting stovepipes making the hill look like the roof of a New England factory. Along the way, Jessie crossed paths with many "go backs," those hapless, disheartened fortune-hunters whose fortunes were not to be found in Marmot Gulch and who thus auctioned their belongings to passersby to afford the long trip back to Kansas or Kentucky or wherever it was they had hoped never to return.

Near the top of the gulch, over nine-thousand feet high, lay Redemption, a glorified mining camp really, unable to boast any Georgetown Loop or Hotel de Paris, despite the "opera house" that once hosted the great Edwin Booth and which stood far too close to the Gore Company's #3 smelter. Compared to stodgy Central City or rough and raucous Black Hawk, Redemption was undoubtedly the ugly sibling of the latter. On its outskirts were the huddled dwellings of the Chinese servants and launderers, the Mexican bloods who usually ended their days shot up or strung up, and those tenacious Cornish miners who made a song of everyday hardship. The ghettos were in unavoidable sight of the rows of low whitewashed cabins housing the majority of women in Redemption—those lost souls whose only real redemption was the gold or silver left on their wash tables after a shift spent working on their backs. Looming high on the hill above the squalor stood several elegant homes, finely detailed and newly painted. Among them one was particularly outstanding, its mansard roofs shingled with scalloped slate in two colors and punctuated with high-windowed dormers. The square tower rising above the hexagonal corner porch came to a point that stabbed the sky, reminding all who passed below of their lot—a townspeople who referred to themselves half-seriously and full of sad irony as the "Redeemed."

"Dried apple pie, ma'am?" The bartender's voice startled Jessie, but she politely declined his offer. She had had more than her fill of that particular dish—along with fried salt pork, muddy coffee, and soda biscuits in greasy gravy—on the coach leaving Ft. Sumner. Then she noticed something amusing.

Three men stood at the far end of the bar. The middle one, taller than the others and blond, was talking briskly and waving his hands. He removed his spectacles and gesticulated over a short stack of thin magazines on the bar before him. His audience, feigning skepticism, was obviously taken by the tall man's spirit. Barely able to hear their words, Jessie made out the tall man to say something like "Guaranteed . . . There's my name, there's where I'm from . . ." The miner closest to her gave in to the sell first with a loud "Awrighty, I'm in! Might could use some hep round here," and pulling a small leather bag from a rear pocket of his denims, he dropped a pinch of gold dust into the tall man's palm. The man on the far side likewise dug for his purse.

The tall man ordered the bartender to serve "these two gents" some beer, and proceeded to slap their backs real friendly-like and shake them at the shoulders. As the first miner replaced the leather bag in his pocket, the tall man's hand discreetly removed it again while he proposed a toast to "dying filthy rich." Jessie watched in awe as the pickpocket expertly inverted the bag in his own jacket pocket then returned it to the miner's without the poor sap suspecting a thing. The thief then lifted and replaced the second man's

19

purse just as smoothly, and with a gallantly tossed coin paid for their beer and headed for the door, urging his two happy customers to go farther west and bidding them farewell. Passing Jessie, his eyes met hers and he cocked his head, mouthing a soft, "Ma'am."

Jessie had to laugh to herself, figuring such business must be routine in these parts. The two hoodwinked miners riffled through the pages of their new purchases, yammering on about grubstakes and the treasures still unfound in Utah. From behind the taps, the barkeep asked Jessie if she'd like anything else. She asked if she might peruse one of the magazines left by the tall gentleman.

A thin booklet, its cover read: "*Johnston's Guide to the Mineral Treasures of the Great Basin, Being a Scientific Appraisal of Geologic Formations and Precious Deposits to Be Found Thereunder, Guaranteed Accurate*, by Cole Johnston, Telluride, Colorado, Geologist in Extremis, Graduate Summa Cum Honoraria, University of Bonn, Price Seventy-five Cents." This was a hoot to Jessie. She had not only heard of such guides to instant riches but also knew phony Latin when she saw it. As she handed it back to the barkeep, her laughter was interrupted by someone calling her name from outside the open door.

"I do apologize for losing you this way."

"Arvilla!" Jessie said, "You found me."

Miss Jessup seemed reluctant to enter the Touchstone. She was like a bird watching for predators. Jessie thanked the barkeep and met Arvilla with a friendly, concerned hug and kiss on the cheek.

"I'm so sorry I wasn't there to meet you," Arvilla sputtered. "The Pinnacles—it just happened the other night."

Arvilla Jessup, thinner and slightly shorter than Jessie, had a fire in her dark eyes that contrasted with her seemingly frail countenance. Her chestnut brown hair hung just below her jaw with barely a wave and with a deep luster that shined even on this hazy afternoon. Her smooth, pale skin was clear and supple right down to her small, pearlike breasts which poked their dark nipples through the white cotton shirt beneath her open black jacket. She was a natural beauty, not gorgeous, but lithe and fit as a doe. The unladylike mud on her high boots reminded Jessie of Arvilla's strong-headed will, her unassuming nature to be just who she wanted to be, never pandering to what people said a young woman should be. She was her own person and Jessie's old friend since their school days in West Texas. "There was just no way to warn you while you were traveling . . ."

"Warn me about what?" Jessie asked. "The hotel isn't important."

Arvilla appeared distressed and wrung her hands. With watering eyes she thanked Jessie emphatically for coming, and with mouth drawn tight, she squelched an urge to cry. She seemed as distraught as Jessie expected anyone to be who had just lost her father. She nodded absently when Jessie affirmed she would have come in any case. As Jessie placed a reassuring hand on Arvilla's arm, a white-bearded gentleman dressed in a black suit stood respectfully by a buckboard, hat in hand, and cleared his throat.

"Oh! Jessie, I'd like for you to meet Judge Atwood. Judge, this is—"

"Miss Jessica Starbuck, of course," he anticipated. "A pleasure. Jefferson Davis Atwood," he said, shaking her hand. "Arvilla has told me many fine things about you—though the Starbuck name is by no means unfamiliar to me." He explained that Arvilla was staying at his ranch house for the time being, her own home harboring too many painful memories.

Arvilla downplayed the fatherly role Judge Atwood had assumed since her father's disappearance, and the old judge politely interrupted to suggest moving off the busy street. His invitation for Jessie to take lodging at his ranch was accepted, but only for one night, as she wanted to spend some time with Arvilla and professed to have some business to conduct in town.

"So be it then," said Atwood, "but we had best make headway. The ranch—I'm sorry to say, Jessie, after your long journey—is more than two hours distant. We shall talk while riding? Fine. Allow me to help you . . ."

Descending through Marmot Gulch the way Jessie had arrived gave the two women time to reacquaint themselves, to retell stories that took them back to their girlhood. At first riding with her arm around her grieving friend, Jessie soon settled into silence, holding Arvilla's cool hand as they traveled amid the indescribable grandeur of an early Colorado sunset. The skies were everywhere more crystal than those over Redemption, allowing Jessie to feast her eyes on the ridged slopes of a great flat-peaked range falling into shadow. Wisps of low cloud clung to the tops of tall lodgepole pines standing ever erect. Before long, Jessie and Arvilla were sharing a blanket against the rapidly cooling twilight air.

"The Pinnacles had running water indoors," Arvilla said apologetically. "Hot and cold. And indoor johnnies, too! Dad and I stayed there once, when we first came . . ."

When Jessie was certain the sentence wouldn't be finished, she said, "You've told me your father disappeared without a trace. There's always the possibility at least that he'll turn up."

"Don't fool yourself, Jessie. The cabin was a wreck. It's been over two weeks. They wouldn't let him live."

"Who?" Jessie asked. "You said no one knew anything."

"No one and everyone, and everyone ain't talking. Ain't that right, Judge?"

Atwood's raised eyebrows gave a silent yes.

"That whole goddamn town knows what's going on and who's doing it."

"What's going on? Who?" Jessie asked in frustration.

Arvilla lashed out. "Open your eyes, girl! Look at that godawful place. Everything is Padgett and Gore." As quickly as she had exploded, Arvilla apologized. She tried to explain more calmly. "Dad cold knew they were fixing the

22

assays. That Keepsake and Valhalla and Never Sleep, those holes are nothing but gangue. Worthless and getting worse. That Padgett's so crooked I'd venture his pecker whistles when he pees—sorry, Judge, but it's true. All they do is get bigger and bigger, that Gore Company, snatching up the small claims—consolidating, they call it, but I'll bet a silver ingot none of them small owners wanted to sell and some of them never really did."

" 'Cept me, of course," chimed in Atwood. He added that he and Arvilla's father and their own geologist had determined that the parcel he sold would probably never return any investment. The Gore Company had the resources to extract the most rebellious ores from the contentious mines; Atwood's small outfit didn't.

When Jessie insisted that Arvilla go to the law, Arvilla replied that no proof could be found. Even if it could, she doubted there was anyone in town interested in throwing down against the man who paid their wages—or their bribes. And the town marshal?

"Virgil Nettles?" Arvilla said and smirked. She exhaled loudly and shook her head. "That walking whiskey barrel's ascared of his own guns, that old fool."

Arvilla's story sounded to Jessie like one long in the making. It portrayed her father, Orrum, as a well-meaning man of principle, clean-living since swearing off the hooch. But Arvilla had suspected her father was under enough pressure to backslide, although she never saw it. He would talk to her sometimes, when the tension became too great to bear alone, when he would sit with his elbows on his knees in the dimly lit cabin cluttered with cracker tins and sledgehammers, turning his wedding ring round and round his finger. As an independent assayer, her father stood much to lose should he be discredited by a reputable firm like Gore Mining and Milling. Had it not been for Atwood's Grand River Mining Company, Arvilla and her father would probably have had to move on once more . . . and he would probably have lived.

23

When Arvilla described the night she thought her father was writing his Last Will, her shaking voice and sniffles drew tears from Jessie as she recalled her own losses. Orrum, being a proud man, had chased Arvilla away when she asked what he was writing, but living in a cramped, two-room shack, it was impossible for the young woman not to notice her father's hand trembling. Among his papers and records after he disappeared, Arvilla had found the card of a mortician who sold coffins in town.

"He knew it was coming. He must have," Arvilla sobbed.

Against a sky of midnight blue, the silhouettes of two hills parted and a valley welcomed them. Farther on, Jessie spied the warm, golden glow that said "home" shining in a short row of windows within a copse of trees. If it hadn't been for the rugged high country, she could have thought she were back at the Circle Star. Passing beneath a high arched gate, the buckboard circled in front of the two-story house, and Jessie was grateful when light from the opening front door spilled upon her. A soft-voiced middle-aged woman greeted them, had a brief word with Atwood, then rushed off to prepare some hot food for the arrivals. A teenaged stable boy took the wagon out back, where he unhitched the team and watered them in stables connected to the main house by an enclosed passage that housed a scullery, a spring, and some storage.

The Atwood ranch was a grand affair in its modest way: Beyond a porch entrance of field stones, wide planks made up the floors; above, timbered rafters of enormous girth supported a steeply pitched roof through which rose a stone chimney on one side of the room and a stovepipe on the other. Most of building was constructed of log, with framed and clapboard extensions to the rear.

Arvilla floated about like a specter—gaunt, quiet, brooding—and Jessie tried not to dote on her too much. While the bereaved girl and Jessie climbed the stairs to their rooms, Rosilda, Atwood's middle-aged domestic, spoke in a low voice with the snowy-haired judge beside the glowing fireplace. Jessie's attention was stolen. She thought nothing of it until later, while at the table, when she sensed that the old man and Arvilla weren't paying much attention to the account of her journey. When she changed course by stating she intended to meet Padgett face-to-face, Arvilla put down her fork and gulped.

"I'm going to see him about supplying pig iron to our shipping concerns—not that I really need to. I just want to get a feel for him."

Atwood cleared his throat and said, "Miss Starbuck, I realize you came a very long way to help your friend in a very difficult time, but I'm not convinced this is something you should involve yourself with too deeply, especially since you're truly far removed from what goes on in Redemption."

"All the better," she responded. She could hide behind her neutrality as a stranger, albeit one who commanded respect on account of the sizeable business she represented. Chances were very good that Padgett was already familiar with the Starbuck name. Putting Atwood's concerns at ease wasn't going to be simple, but she was obliged to find some way to help. She assured her host that she would not "get in too deep." Atwood was not appeased.

Arvilla said, more as a statement than a question, "There were men here again tonight, weren't there?" Atwood merely nodded. Jessie's inquiring eyes induced Arvilla to explain, "Strangers have been sighted this past week or so along the property lines here and around the switchbacks across the ridge." To Atwood she said, "I heard Darnell talking. I know you didn't want to worry me, Judge, but I ain't deaf, blind, or too delicate."

Atwood denied that there had been any trouble. The trespassers were just noodling around some quartz leads and outcrops, but Arvilla was aware that the strangers were from Redemption. Their soiled miner's clothes and boots were a dead giveaway. Atwood was already sending armed outriders to secure the property. So far it was a peaceable tension. The last thing he wanted was blood spilled on either side. Arvilla said she wouldn't mind that one bit as long as it weren't their own. She might even be inclined herself to help the matter along, "begging the Judge's pardon, as I am his guest."

Jessie was pleased to know this was the same old gutsy Arvilla Jessup who had once punched out an ill-bred, shameless young cowpoke twice her size, back when she and Jessie were spreading their wings. It was over a private little incident Jessie herself had witnessed that held not a little embarrassment for at least two of the people involved, the brazen buck especially. The thought of the affair made Jessie smile to herself, startled by such an off-color story coming to mind while at the table of her refined host. But it was an episode Jessie just had to relive with Arvilla, just for the laugh.

Beneath the low, slanting ceiling of Arvilla's bedroom after saying their good nights, Jessie giggled as she closed the door behind Arvilla, saying, "You have not changed one iota, girl." Not understanding what Jessie was getting at, but succumbing to her contagious smile, Arvilla let Jessie sit her on the edge of the high bed, wondering why her Texan friend had such a mischievous look in her eye. When Jessie explained, Arvilla had to laugh at herself, placing a hand to her throat with emotion, it felt so good.

"What was that boy's name? Keefe?"

"Yep," Jessie said. "The one who grew like a weed the year he spent on Daddy's range and was after me like a bull in heat."

"That boy was so-o-o fine—until he opened his dumb mouth."

They guffawed as each recalled her own side of the story, a simple one that Jessie was satisfied to leave certain details out of, but which she couldn't help imagining. She remembered that it had taken place during the spring roundup. She and Arvilla were the favorite topic of the cowhands' conversation that season, although the foremen

26

would never allow the boys to show any disrespect. The two of them had the run of the range, as free-spirited as any two fillies could be. Arvilla fell for a handsome colt in time, a good fellow who treated her right—both in the light of day among friends and in the glow of the camp fire by night alone. Then there was Keefe, who had an eye for Jessie's obvious charms but who never commanded her interest.

Jessie and Keefe were alike in their hardheadedness. They competed in every way, especially in riding, and neither was a graceful loser. The more they locked horns, it seemed, the more Keefe's desire for Jessie was fired, and after a while, Jessie began believing that perhaps this lanky wrangler's ardent attentions were genuine affection . . . until the day they went to the barn together for some feed and stumbled upon Arvilla and her beau naked from the waist down and smack in the middle of something hot and heavy.

At the sight of Arvilla straddling her man, her well-rounded rump spread wide, rising and falling in the rhythm of erotic passion, Jessie turned away without embarrassment. She was secure with her own sexuality and at home with the naturalness of sex.

Arvilla had her head buried in her lover's shoulder, and they were moaning loudly. The cowpoke pushed his heels into the hay to better thrust his stiffly engorged cock into Arvilla's overflowing vagina, her soft, pink labia sliding smoothly along the veined shaft and stretching in and out with it on each deep penetration. The long, black tangle of pubic hair that extended well back along her most intimate crease was drenched with her juices and clung to her perfect skin. His hands probed her luscious ass, squeezing by turns the bouncing flesh, dimpling it with his fingertips and reaching down to spread her sex wider. Arvilla bucked insatiably, curving her pelvis forward and back while lifting and falling upon her man's erection, taking it in as far as it would go then gyrating upon it with all her weight. The excitement soon became unbearable for the reclining

27

wrangler, and as his scrotum tightened, his groans became grunts, and he spent himself in a thrashing convulsion, arching his back to deepen his lunge. The excitement was too much for Keefe, too, and in his clumsy maneuvering for a better view, he knocked a bridle from its hook upon the wall, spoiling the game for all. He bolted just as Arvilla and her lover looked up.

They couldn't tell whose back it was they had glimpsed darting behind the swaying bridles. That secret was given away by the voyeur himself a day later when Keefe approached the sexy Miss Jessup as she relaxed beneath a cottonwood, watching the sunset. Jessie never knew exactly what it was Keefe said to Arvilla, and the teasing lass wouldn't tell, but it was clear that Keefe's overture was unwelcome and rude. When he groped for her breasts and moved to unbuckle his belt, Arvilla reflexively elbowed him in the gut, spun to her feet, and nailed a stone-hard fist across the bridge of his nose, flattening it across his face and making it bleed too much for him to be interested in anything but hightailing it out of there.

" . . . But not before I landed a muddy bootprint square on his haunch for all his bean-eating buddies to see," Arvilla added with a smile.

Soon her smile faded. Nothing could seem very funny for long to her. She and the world had lost a good man, her father, leaving the balance burdened with the kind of men who took him away. It was as difficult for Arvilla to talk as it was for her to do anything but sit and remember and cry. Jessie's quiet company seemed to please her, so when Jessie suggested they retire to their separate rooms, Arvilla's hand was reluctant to release Jessie's as they parted.

Through the impenetrable silence that descended when Jessie doused her lamp, faces came to her that were difficult to see clearly—faces of her father and the folks back home. She was saddened by the realization that it was becoming harder as the years elapsed to recall the sound

28

of her father's voice. She imagined hearing someone else call her name, someone dear to her, who by his presence made her feel safe. Someone who was no longer very far away . . . *Ki.*

★

Chapter 3

He called himself Ki. Unless one were to have scrutinized him closely and seen the Asian folds of his eyes, he could not have been mistaken for anything but Caucasian. However, in the past there had been some who wondered what Indian nation he belonged to, since his long, straight hair had the blue-black tint many natives shared. He was half-Japanese, sired by an American "barbarian" and therefore an outcast among his own people—as was his high-born mother, who lost her noble position in Japanese society when she took her Western husband. And so, Ki had nothing much more than bitterness—no resources beyond the nearly limitless store of energy he discovered in himself during his time spent in a monastery; nothing beyond the "spirit meeting" in his heart that led him to take the name "Ki," or beyond his mastery of martial arts that served him in conflict—and which could prove deadly when unleashed.

But Ki seldom unleashed such power; instead, he focused it toward good use in the service of the man who had befriended his family long ago, Alex Starbuck, and the beautiful Starbuck girl, Jessie. This was Ki's duty as a warrior, his debt as a friend, ever since he exiled himself from his mother's homeland. It was this duty that now brought him to Redemption riding a half-lame hired mule, clothed in the ill-fitting jacket, high black Wellingtons, and heavy denim trousers that marked him as a miner.

Melpomene Hall, hautily referred to as the "opera house," stood haggard beneath a pall of smoke rising from the number three smelter that stood on higher ground close by. Behind the opera house about thirty men loitered. They wore brightly colored uniforms that caught Ki's attention: white pants, blue military-style waistcoats—some bearing stripes on the sleeves—blue caps, and red bandannas knotted about their necks. They stood lazily alongside teamsters who minded two teams of enormous draft horses hitched to sturdy, deep-bodied wagons. Heavy, thick-beamed crates were being loaded by workers who looked too frail to handle them. Ki watched until his eyes met those of a young, mustachioed guard who sat atop a barrel, pawing the barrel of his upright carbine. Ki figured it was smelted ore the men were guarding, refined and ready to make its journey to someone's coffers in San Francisco or Denver. Somewhere other than Redemption.

Nudging his lethargic mule onward, Ki proceeded up Eagle Road, feeling peaked, hungry, and somewhat lost, yet knowing what he needed to do. Suspicious eyes followed him until he came to Gillis's Dry Goods shop, where he dismounted and tethered the animal. Gillis's was a dimly lit establishment overcrowded with hardware of every description. The aisles were choked with toppling piles of denims, stacks of tins and bottles, bundles of rope, and racks of picks, shovels, spikes, and chisels. One wall consisted of dozens of rectangular bins, each filled with some useful and sorely overpriced sundry such as candles and oil lamps, flint and gunpowder. Flour sold at the exorbitant price of twenty-five dollars per hundred pounds. And though Gillis was a purveyor of dry goods, he saw his way clear to selling gallons of local whiskey, "Guaranteed to kill at 40 rods," at a hefty eight dollars each. The sound of boot heels upon the plank floor told Ki there were several people in the place, though he only saw two standing in the aisle before him, one of whom was the tall, bespectacled blond just completing a successful sale of his prospectors' guides to Mr. Gillis himself. It was a few awkward moments before Gillis shook the tall man's extended hand, and he looked bothered doing it, mumbling, "Fine, Mister . . ."

"Johnston," replied the tall blond. "Cole Johnston."

Noticing Ki's wandering eyes—obviously the eyes of a newcomer—Johnston turned to him, holding one of his guides in hand, and when Ki came within arm's length, he raised a friendly hand to pat his new prospect on the shoulder. But his hand fell uselessly through the air as Ki moved from under it as smoothly as water over a fall. Johnston didn't even see the motion, and Ki stood there, expressionless, about to say something, but beaten to it by Johnston's free-flowing sales pitch.

"Now, this here looks like a man who knows some leads when he see 'em. Why, I'll wager you done had your fill of that Black Hills gold and Clear Creek silver by the time them Homestake and Champion people gobbled up all the claims." Ki politely tried to excuse himself, but Johnston's pitch was iron-clad. "So now you're in'erested in heading elsewhere, someplace where there ain't as many miners as there are lodes to be mined. Well, by golly, this little gem of a book tells you just where you'll find the loveliest little blossom rock . . ."

"I'm not a prospector," Ki interrupted. "I'm independently wealthy and just looking to work in the mines as a diversion." He apologized for not being interested in Johnston's guidebook and asked Gillis if he could have a word with him.

"Best of luck to you then, my friend. If you change your mind, Mr. Gillis here has agreed to purvey this unique investment—worth its weight in gold, I tell you that."

The tall blond took his leave with a polite farewell. Gillis shrugged and said he didn't think the book was worth a cow chip, despite his percentage. Gillis struck Ki as the hard-as-nails, straight-shooting type. Judging by his shingle out front marked "Est. 1877," just three years ago, when the Gore Company was turning a tent-and-shanty mining camp into a town, Ki figured the stout, red-faced man for someone not to fool with. Anyone brave enough—or wild enough—to stake his fortune in Marmot Gulch at a time when men were still fighting and dying for virgin soil was no tenderfoot. The open-frame .44 Colt that never left Gillis's side was proof enough. With its solid walnut grips, the weapon was more accurate and harder-hitting than some of its solid-frame rivals. Just like its owner, Ki thought. When Ki asked the proprietor where he might go to find work in the mines, Gillis looked him over carefully, almost with a pitiful look in his eye. He placed his arms akimbo, one hand on his gun.

"Why any man would want to haul hisself down them tunnels to earn his grub I can't figger. Reckon you gonna git rich, do ya?" Ki shook his head and Gillis chuckled. "Forgot. You independent rich," he said and tried not to smile. He explained that the only real work in the gulch was with the Gore Company, which operated well over a dozen headframed mines and one open cut. The company's offices were just up the street; Ki could inquire there or just show up at the wagon yard in the morning and see the shift boss. A man didn't need much skill to work the mines. Just some brawn and nothing left to lose. The pay was meager but steady—if you stayed alive. Ki said he was familiar with the dangers, to which Gillis replied, leaning over his counter and looking closely at the folds of Ki's almond eyes, "Tell me somethin'. You got you hair all long and tied back like a show horse. You talk real fancy, too. You ain't no *real* miner, now are ya?"

"If I weren't no real miner, I mighta been inclined to buy that there get-rich guide. Can you tell me who to talk to?"

Gillis stood back, trying to figure Ki out but satisfied for now.

"Like I said, some boys just show up at the yard. They might know how to work. But I happen to know that the company folk round here, they wanna know if a man can drink. Git yerself to the Lodgepole, crost from the yard. That's where the foremen do their hiring."

"Who should I ask for?"

"A big ol' hoss with black hair all tied back like yours. Name's Benton. Ryde Benton."

As Ki rounded the corner toward the wagon yard, the air was filled with the noise of riot—rumbling sounds of wooden furniture falling and smashing, glass shattering, men yelling and cursing, and finally, gunshots, muffled and flat, and the wild neighing of horses—but none of it could be seen on the streets. Ki had paused to gauge the danger when suddenly the butterfly doors on the Lodgepole Saloon burst open, slamming hard against the door posts, and three men came tumbling to the ground followed by three others on their feet. More gunshots and heavy pounding from within accompanied the yelling of patrons as the doors smashed open again, this time to belch forth three raucous, rearing stallions, the riders firing their guns at the ceiling. Bottles flew through the air, missing their mounted targets and smashing into the street. The riders reigned in their spooked horses and fired harmless parting shots into the Lodgepole sign. The ejected men on the ground found their feet and scattered, and several other patrons flowed from the door hurling curses and the legs of bar stools at the fleeing riders. Still others stood by, doubling over with laughter. Just the conclusion to another late-afternoon losing spree at the gambling tables, if Ki was a fair judge of such goings on, and he was. He had seen plenty such behavior in his far-flung travels with Jessie. Cow towns and mining towns, this was their nature. Throw together fortune hunters with time and fast money on their hands, add a little whiskey and guns, and it makes for a darned

34

explosive mix. As he had seen it happen elsewhere, things quieted down soon enough. Ki entered the hell-for-leather barrel house while overturned tables and chairs were righted and new decks of cards were shuffled. A group of men in the front corner tried to calm down one man with plenty of fight left in him, and business went on as usual. Removing his floppy hat, Ki stepped to the bar, where it was obvious the ruckus hadn't disrupted several men's drinking one bit.

The barkeep, a ruddy-faced young man with a Cornish accent, greeted Ki with a lively hello, keeping one eye on the quarrel continuing at the corner table. Ki ordered a beer and made small talk about the horses. The voices behind Ki grew louder still. Handing Ki his mug of foaming brew, the bartender finally yelled across the room, "Now, keep it light there, or I'll haf to ask ya's all to leave, I will." He apologized to Ki and complained that the ruffians made the Lodgepole their primary residence. "I never saw such t'ings back home," he said, his voice lilting with melody. " 'Tis a bloody disgrace, it is."

Ki put down his money, dropped an eye-opening tip, and inquired where he might find Ryde Benton. The barkeep dipped his head toward the clutch of men standing at the bar, saying, "Ye might ask these fellas here. They could help, I'm sure."

"Pardon me, fellas," said Ki, "could you point me to Ryde Benton?"

There were four men nursing drinks and talking quietly. They turned in unison toward the newcomer who stood nearly a full head taller than any of them.

"On what business?" said the scrawniest one.

"Getting work . . . in the hole."

"I'm Benton," the scrawny one said. "You can talk to me."

Not the "big ol' hoss" Gillis had described. This guy hadn't seen fresh milk or green vegetables since puberty, and his skin obviously itched and burned. He had scratched his forearm raw. Some such miners treated themselves with calamine. Others used large doses of alcohol internally. He asked Ki nothing about mining; rather, where was he from, how old was he, did he own a horse? Ki told him he was from around Animas, but had just come from a failed operation in the Medicine Bows. After the man had raised his empty whiskey glass to his parched lips twice, Ki got the message and offered to buy him a round.

"Darn good o' you t'ask. I believe I'll take a double."

Reaching into his trouser pocket, Ki paused and said, "So when do you think I can start?"

The man fidgeted and said, "Now, don't be in any kinda rush, son. There be stockyards full o' able-bodied muckers in this town."

Ki had removed an empty hand and suggested he had better find the company office instead when the man tried to pull Ki's jacket open to check for weapons. Ki snapped the man's hand in a vice-like hold before the jacket opened. He warned the scarecrow that it was impolite to reach for a man's personals for any reason. His cold stare and powerful grip surprised his acquaintance and convinced him to release the material, but Ki noticed the other men looking toward the tables against the wall. The thin man assured Ki it would be wiser to let him go, if he were to find any work in Redemption.

Ki let him go easy. Dropping two bits on the bar, he called out, "Barkeep, a single shot of whatever my friend here is drinking."

As the man raised his glass, he turned his back to the bar, trying to appear casual as he scanned the room before him. Ki followed his eyes to a table near the potbellied stove corner where sat two men, one of them likely to be the "big ol' hoss" Gillis had told of. Ki focused on the big man to draw his attention. He didn't need to try so hard. The big man, realizing that Ki knew who he was, gave a faint nod to the scrawny one, who slugged down his drink and said, "Over here . . ."

36

All the while the men up front had barely been able to quiet the angry one, who continued to drink and argue about winning fair and square over that "jacklegged coyote" who stole his money. As the scrawny man led Ki to the table at the rear, no one seemed to care the least bit about the argument. The thin man stood before the table with Ki, saying, "He wants to work."

The big man with the black ponytail and colorless eyes stared a moment then said, "Thanks, Kyle . . . I'm Ryde Benton. How can I help you?" Ki looked at the impersonator, who slinked back to the bar with a wink and a smile.

As Ki again explained himself to Benton, trying to make every detail match his first story, two men at the front table had had enough and were redrawing the battle lines in a hail of threats and cussing. As Ki spoke, the fight erupted in full force, bringing the young Cornish barkeep over the bar and into the fray, to prove himself a bartender who kept his word. After landing terrible, jarring blows upon one man, then the other, he single-handedly threw them both headlong from the Lodgepole to taste the moist Redemption dust.

Neither Benton nor his pard acknowledged the brawl, but stared intently at Ki, who remained standing in front of them. All was silent while Benton scrutinized the tall, lean man before him. When he finally spoke, it was wind through a narrow canyon.

"We could always use new muckers. You'll start out doing that, and if you're good, we'll get you double-jacking or tramming ore cars. Be at the yard an hour past sunup— come as you are." Reaching into his vest pocket, he said, "Give this to the pit foreman and tell him what I said. His name's Boyd," and handed Ki his card.

"Obliged," Ki responded. "Also, could you tell me where I might find a bed?"

"Sure," he said and then called to the scrawny one. "Kyle! Show this man to a bed." To Ki he said loudly enough for

37

Kyle to hear, "And don't let him charge you any more than a buck and a half."

All of Redemption passed along Eagle Road.

Leaving the Lodgepole, the abrasive Kyle led Ki downhill, descending through strata of squalor going from bad to worse and then into poverty. The mouth of Marmot Gulch yawned wide below them as horse and pedestrian traffic along the winding road echoed from the scarred hills. The high afternoon sun was finally burning through the dun cloud cover as Ki noticed a buckboard drawn by a handsome team rounding the church below.

"Them gopher holes behind the white cabins is where you'll sleep tonight. Then later maybe I can find you something better—but it ain't gonna cost no dollar-fifty," Kyle whined. "You git what you pay fer, y'know."

Slowing his pace to nearly a standstill, Ki watched the long honey-blond tresses of the woman passenger become more distinct, more attractive, as she rode beside her teen-aged driver. The horses' hides gleamed with sweat, and their bridles bore the simple monogram of the Atwood ranch on small circular escutcheons. As the team passed, Ki locked his sights upon Jessie's incomparable green eyes, fully understanding Jessie's avoidance of anything more than a subtle glance toward her longtime friend and protector.

"Give it up, pard," said Kyle. "She ain't gonna look at the likes of you twice. You can see she ain't nothin' but a uppity Atwood bitch."

The hair on Ki's neck bristled.

Seeing the buckboard recede, Kyle added, "Mmm, but I do declare. I wouldn't mind splittin' her like a roast chicken!"

"She'd kill a twerp like you."

Thrusting one arm into Ki's shoulder, Kyle hissed, "What you goddamn say?" but Ki easily deflected him and pulled his arm along, using Kyle's strength against him. He threw the scrawny pest off balance to slide to his knees in the

38

mud. Leaping to his feet with fists clenched, Kyle's first reaction was to attack, but seeing Ki's stance of unmistakable readiness, he thought better of it and shook off the mud instead.

"You find yerself y'own goddamn bed," he spat and stormed off with finger wagging, "and you jest watch out in that hole tomorra, hear me? You jest watch yerself."

★

Chapter 4

In the short time it took Jessie to book a room at the Caribou Hotel—a seedy, third-rate hovel and the only choice remaining in town—it seemed Redemption was on the verge of a rush. Stepping out to the boardwalk, she discovered a crowd outside the offices of *The Telegraph*, Redemption's weekly newspaper, housed in a two-story clapboard with a brick facade. The growing mob spilled across the road, choking it closed amid dogs barking and the cacophony of steam whistles and stamp mills. Young men ran past Jessie, barely taking notice of her shapely legs and hips accentuated by the tight, broken-in denim Levi's she wore. Calling out to a miner running by, Jessie asked what the commotion was. All he could do was point to the tramway on the mountain above and yell, "Somethin's goin' on at the Never Sleep!" A man trotting next to him added, "It's a strike! They done struck paydirt!" Jessie peered up the hill to see the long tramway used to transport men and light equipment up and down the steep, treeless rise, which never stood still night or day, yet was now motionless, its steam engine idling within its shed. Across the distance she had no difficulty recognizing the red, white, and blue uniforms of the militia men guarding the approaches to the Never Sleep.

Never a dull moment in this town, she thought just as a messenger boy exited the hotel, looked at the crowd down the street, then at Miss Starbuck, and dashed off toward the luxurious homes at the top of the hill. He was on his way to deliver Jessie's calling card to Mr. C. C. Padgett at his home overlooking the frenzied mining camp. Jessie hoped to meet with him there later that day. Like everything in remote mining towns, where the simplest commodity was a luxury, the dispatch was pricey—a dollar more than the two or three bits it would have cost elsewhere. Even her room at the Caribou made her wince, being a musty, low-ceilinged apartment costing nearly a miner's day wage in an establishment that rented rooms with or without beds. She insisted on having a front room with windows overlooking the street, and secured one only with an additional outlay of gold coin.

She headed toward *The Telegraph* to find out more. About to step off the boardwalk to cross the street, she noticed the "geologist in extremis," Cole Johnston, forlornly gathering into a canvas satchel his guidebooks, now forgotten by the fortune hunters rushing toward the newspaper. Beside him, a grizzled, defeated-looking man, undoubtedly half as old as he looked, was pleading for the tall blond to sell him one. There was no mistaking that the old prospector was a go-back. The pile of personal belongings and castoffs loosely assembled on a travois would have told the story even had it not been for the hand-painted cloth sign reading, "Busted by God!" Weapons, shovels, picks, spare shirts, and boots, all badly worn and dirty, were there for auction— even his tired burro—likely at a tenth of their original cost, by a man whom the mountains had beaten. Still, the poor sod held out his bits, probably among his last, to the tall geologist who represented some distant hope, however unrealistic, that fortune awaited all those who persisted. Standing behind the corner of the building, Jessie

41

watched the transaction in complete surprise as Johnston shoved back the old man's hand, refusing to take any money. She heard him say, "Save it, old man, and forget these books. If there was any gold in them hills, you'd have found your share by now." She watched in some amazement as Johnston, donning a wide-brimmed suede hat, insisted that his books were worthless and forced a half eagle into the old prospector's shirt pocket, demanding that he not gamble it and to beat it out of Redemption as soon as possible. The handsome pickpocket wasn't all scallywag after all, Jessie realized. He only bamboozled the hardcases and mule-headed saddle scum who, in his mind, deserved being parted from their ill-gotten gains. Scurrying across the street, Jessie skirted the mob before Johnston left the go-back.

The crowd was dense with gossip about what was happening five hundred feet below the surface in the Never Sleep mine. Names of friends and brothers and fathers on the overnight shift who remained underground were bandied about as if they were either privileged or dead. Jessie stood on her toes to see if there was any movement at the doors of *The Telegraph*. What caught her eye instead was the handsome tanned hat of the geologist above the heads of the miners. He turned to her, caught her staring, and smiled. Jessie dropped to her heels. When she stole another glance, he was approaching.

Removing his hat to catch the sunshine in his hair, he said, "Quite a show, I expect." Jessie's response wasn't much more than a smile and a nod, putting the play back in his hands. "Any news from Frisco yet?"

"I just got here," she said. "I don't even know what's going on."

"Lock-in, I reckon. Seen 'em before."

Just then a surge in the mob threw the two of them against each other, and the tall geologist suggested they step back from the crush. The satchel he carried, stuffed with his booklets, also held various tools and odd pieces of hardware. He explained to Jessie that a lock-in could mean two things: Either the miners had uncovered a mother lode that would send the company stock soaring and were trying to keep it secret a while, or, more likely, the company was just pretending that's what had happened, to inflate the stock value.

"That doesn't sound legal," Jessie interjected.

"Ain't no law against speculatin', ma'am," he replied. "But it's a might underhanded, sure enough."

After an uncomfortable silence, the geologist suddenly offered his hand to Jessie, apologizing for being rude, and formally introduced himself: "John Coleson, ma'am, at your service. I recall seeing you yesterday in the Touchstone."

Jessie's tilted head and wry smile made him uneasy. She slowly shook his large hand, excited by the warm energy of his firm, gentle grip.

"Mr. Coleson," Jessie affirmed. She stared at him a second longer. "Jessica Starbuck. Yes, I do recall seeing you in the Touchstone. I believe you were trading in— what was it?—guides to mineral treasures?"

The tall blond blushed and briefly checked the ground he hoped had not shifted beneath him.

"Oh, that . . . Yes, that is one source of income I've been pursuing . . ."

"Are there many others, Mr. *Coleson*?"

"If I may explain, Miss Starbuck—" Touching her elbow, he guided her farther away from the townsmen, his ears now fiery red.

"Do explain, please, Mr. Coleson. Or is it Johnston?"

"John Coleson is my true name. You see, the nature of the publishing world is such . . . that is, there are certain markets that are, shall I say, advantageous for certain types of work . . ."

"Or, shall we say, exploitative?" Jessie jibed. Keeping an eye on the crowd, she spotted Ki standing on the far side of the street.

Coleson stammered, "The truth is, *Johnston's Guide* is not the most reputable publication—but not altogether disreputable, either. The information in it was quite solid . . . at one time . . . and it could be useful, in principle . . ."

Jessie's smirk was as magnetic as it was off-putting. She folded her arms, and Coleson was almost certain he sensed her foot tapping.

"It ain't uncommon for authors like myself to use made-up names, you understand." Finally, in surrender, he said, "I take no pride in the book, Miss Starbuck, but it is an open market. 'Let the buyer beware.' A man's got to earn his keep and—"

"Mr. Coleson," she interrupted, "you don't need to explain yourself to me. I learned long ago that people should believe nothing they hear and only half of what they read. . . . Perhaps nothing in the case of your book, of course."

Although she couldn't approve of Coleson's lifestyle, Jessie couldn't deny the attraction she felt for him. The muscular forearms exposed beneath his rolled-up shirtsleeves pointed to a man in fine condition, not a shiny-butt egghead who shirked hard work. His chiseled features and deep-set eyes of hazel spoke of character, and his manner was obviously poised and learned. The slight bow to the solid columns that were his legs and the narrow, toe-worn boots indicated a horseman and possibly even a good one. She wondered if he had got his handsome tan by collecting rock samples and fossils—if he were really a geologist—or by earning his keep on horseback. She was intrigued by the mystery surrounding him, being always wary of the lizard-bellied swindlers common to every mining camp in creation. She was vague about how long she intended to remain in town when he inquired, but more clear when he invited her to supper at the Touchstone.

"Thank you, Mr. Coleson, but another time would be more convenient." Shaking his hand, she bade him farewell, adding, "I'm sure we'll be crossing paths again soon."

44

In the same way that morning came late to Redemption because of the high surrounding peaks, so evening came early in the afternoon. Standing on the hexagonal porch of the Padgett mansion, waiting to be admitted, Jessie held the collar of her dress closed against the stiffening breeze. From this vantage point she could see almost all of Redemption spread below in the shadowed valley. The crowd on the main street had dispersed some time ago; only a few stragglers remained outside *The Telegraph*. The contrast between the spacious, ornate homes of the mine executives and successful merchants atop the gulch and the squalid tents and makeshift clapboard apartments of the workers below seemed more conspicuous when one took it all in at once.

Through the faceted bevels of the cut and frosted glass in the door, Jessie saw the distorted figure of a man approach. The great portal swung open to reveal a handsome young butler with neatly trimmed black hair and well-tailored suit. His "Good afternoon, may I help you?" struck Jessie as befitting any of the finest households in San Francisco or Galveston. She introduced herself and was led across a thick burgundy carpet on a landing beneath the most magnificent staircase she had seen in a long while.

While the town of Redemption was generally a town not of conspicuous spending, but rather of steady hard work and insecurity, the Padgett mansion was the exception in its gaudy display of splendor. Estimating there to be at least twenty-five rooms, Jessie was awed by the vast hallway lined with ancient Chinese urns, amber gas-lit sconces, and lush cherrywood walls. High above the open stair a rosette window allowed a flood of white light to bathe the high expanse in which hung an enormous crystal chandelier. At the edge of the carpet, the floor was an alternating pattern of maple and mahogany, shined to a high gloss. The butler helped Jessie remove her shawl and hung it carefully in a hallway cabinet. "This way, please," he said with barely a glance at the lovely visitor, who wore a simple, elegant gray silk dress with a low-cut bodice that accented her sun-browned cleavage.

The butler led her through an archway into the sitting room beyond, appointed with red silk wall covering and a high rectangular mirror. He pulled open a curtained pair of glass-paned doors sliding in a curved trace and stood to one side, indicating that Jessie was to enter the drawing room within. At the far end of the portrait-lined chamber sat a pale, diminutive man in a black, high-collared suit. Sitting beside a rolling service cart carrying a silver samovar, he did not rise immediately, but ran one finger beneath his small, curved mustache, somewhat nervously. He stood and with a slight bow said, "Miss Starbuck, please—"

He offered her a plush chair beside the circular table before him and asked if she had eaten. He suggested she try the remarkable oysters his cook specialized in—remarkable, indeed, Jessie thought, over a thousand miles from the sea. She accepted instead his offer of tea and cake, served by Lance, the butler. The service was meticulously formal— white gloves, silver utensils, silk serviettes embossed with the letters C. C. P. Padgett directed Lance to close the doors as he left.

Padgett gorged himself on one small piece of cake after another during the initial formalities. All that came to Jessie's mind when Padgett asked her, "How do you like my prosperous little kingdom?" was the word "stupefying."

"I'm stunned." she said. "The scenery, the remoteness . . . this house!"

"I would expect so, Miss Starbuck. Now, I understand your family's shipping concerns have a long-standing relationship with various suppliers east of here. What brings you to Redemption?"

With utmost professionalism, Jessie outlined the need of her various holdings for high-grade iron in the construction of ships and railways in America and abroad. During the discussion, Padgett listened quietly, pinching pieces of cake with his slender fingers and swallowing them with little chewing. Jessie noticed the portliness he hid so well beneath his expensive clothing. She explained that she was investigating various suppliers in the region capable of providing what she needed, and when she mentioned the Grand River Mining Company, Padgett's prejudice was thinly veiled by his strained politeness.

"Third-rate, at best. Diligent producers though they are— and a fine man, Atwood—I assure you, Grand River's product is sorely inferior to ours, their output irregular. They would never meet your demands as well as we would."

"I was under the impression that iron production was secondary to the Gore Company's interests in precious metals," Jessie probed.

"And still we outproduce Grand River."

His agitation was increasingly evident with each reference to his arch rival, so Jessie shifted the subject somewhat now that she had him talking. As their conversation unfolded, the portrait of Padgett Jessie had was of a man ill at ease among people, especially the "ignorant muckers" who drove his industry and his very lifestyle. His imperious demeanor Jessie suspected was a blind for his inward shyness and insecurity. His eccentricity was apparent, as when he wiped his teaspoon clean after each stirring of his tea or in the way he obsessively brushed from his lap crumbs that weren't there. His most normal moment, perhaps, was when, with eyes lingering on Jessie's voluptuous breasts, he asked if she was married. What a pity, it seemed to him, that no man should share her obvious "charms." Returning the question of marriage his way, Jessie was struck by his impassive statement that his wife had died "of a wasting disease" years before. It had been so traumatic, he claimed, that he had been unable to remarry ever since. Nevertheless, not the least bit of emotion clouded his eyes or turned his lips. He seemed impervious.

Up to a point.

"So, Mr. Padgett, what's the news from Never Sleep?"

"I'm afraid I don't know what you mean," he said, setting down his cup with a trembling hand.

"There was an enormous crowd of men surrounding the telegraph office at the newspaper earlier. The tramway was at a standstill." Padgett remained expressionless. "There was talk of a lock-in."

Standing abruptly, Padgett crossed the room, ad-libbing without looking her in the eye, playing for time.

"Miss Starbuck, the mining industry is a very unpredictable business. New veins are always being sought as existing ones pay out. At least half the profit from one mine is necessary to fund the sinking of another, and we are constantly prospecting for new opportunities." Finally he turned to face her. "There was blasting going on in Never Sleep last night and this morning. It is standard procedure to withhold all comings and goings during such operations."

"I see," Jessie said. "That explains it."

Rising from her seat, she nonchalantly asked, "Does the Gore Company's board have any hopes of buying out Grand River Mining?"

Padgett blurted, "We won't need to buy that mismanaged hodgepodge. They'll crumble beneath their own weight."

Jessie turned with a surprised look in her eye. "I understand they're doing well."

"I'm sure that's what they would show you on paper, Miss Starbuck, but I assure you, if I—if we buy out their assets, it will only be due to our greater efficiency and resources."

"And what about 'leverage,' Mr. Padgett?"

"That's all I can say on the matter."

She announced it was time to leave and she would appreciate being welcomed to inspect his smelting facilities in the next few days.

He replied as delicately as possible, "Miss Starbuck, it is inconceivable to me that a mere woman would have any understanding of—any interest, that is—in smelting or any other aspect of this industry. If you have further interest in negotiating business, I would highly recommend sending a body of engineers experienced in such matters as needed. As president of Gore Mining and Milling and its major shareholder, I would more than welcome the chance to meet with your man in charge of operations."

Standing close enough to him for him to smell her perfume, Jessie replied, "Mr. Padgett, you're looking at the man in charge. I thank you for your time," and she saw herself to the door. "My shawl, please," she said to Lance.

Following her, Padgett said, "I didn't mean to insult you. It's just that women never . . . I've never dealt with a woman who—"

"If we are to do any business together," Jessie interjected, "perhaps you can find someone who has dealt with women in executive positions."

Padgett's voice elevated to a whine. "I have no problem dealing with women, if only—"

Jessie spun on her heels.

"I never said you did, Mr. Padgett. Relax."

He drew a quick breath and silenced himself. With a weak handshake, he bade Jessie good-bye and watched her figure distort through the cut glass. He muttered the word "bitch" out loud behind the closed door, which also prevented him from hearing Jessie proclaim him a "prize horse's ass."

The town marshal's office, Jessie's next stop, was almost as tiny as a two-horse stall and smelled only slightly better. A rusted wood stove with a poorly sealed pipe crouched in a corner near the door. Against the wall opposite the gun rack stood two cramped jail cells, each barely six-foot square, made of closely crosshatched strap iron. The large oak desk never got dusted except by the butts of people sitting on it, or by the marshal's own shirtsleeves and forehead, as he had a habit of sleeping on it. A waste pail beyond the desk had a halo of balled-up paper lying on the dusty plank floor around it, the failed results of the only target practice the marshal ever tried. Dog-eared sheets of paper were piled inches high atop a cabinet, with crooked drawers sprouting still more paper, as if overfed with the stuff. The place exhibited a free balance between disarray and disorder. Bridles were hung on the same hooks as key rings. Gunbelts beside unwashed tin plates. Moldy hunks of cheese upon stacks of dockets. A slate window sill scattered with handfuls of empty cartridge cases and boxes. Inside a desktop filing bin sat a plate with yesterday's uneaten grilled chicken, thick with flies. This was the scene that greeted Jessie when she opened the unlatched door, her loud knocking having been answered by the marshal saying, "I'm out back! Come on in!" Jessie silently moved to the back door and peeked outside. There he stood, leaning on one arm, urinating on the wall.

"I'll be right th—" he began while turning, wagging his limp, dripping wang for Jessie to see, shaking golden droplets onto his trouser legs and boots. " 'Scuse me," he said without a flinch and turned away, bowing his legs and gyrating his hips as he stowed his gear and buttoned up. Entering his office, he shook a thumb over his shoulder, muttering, " 'Pologies, ma'am. I was just . . . you know." Jessie followed his reddened eyes as they moved up and down her body until he finally introduced himself, "I'm Virge Nettles. The marshal." He extended his hand, suddenly drew it back and wiped it across his large stomach, then extended it again. By that time, Jessie had pulled up a chair, removed the saddle blanket and claw hammer left there, and sat down.

"How do you do, Marshal. I am Jessica Starbuck."

Nettles sputtered with excitement, almost at a loss for words. When he finally managed to say, "I've heard so much about you. Who'd ever imagine you'd hitch up to my post here in Redemption?" he started clearing his desk of rubbish. "What in tarnation brang y'all out this away?"

"I'm a friend of Arvilla Jessup's."

Nettles's face lost some muscle tone with that remark. He drew a wrinkled, liver-spotted hand down his long, white mustache and brushed it from his lips with his knuckles. Averting his eyes, all he could say was that Arvilla's father's disappearance was "damned unrighteous," Jessup being such a good man to Nettles's reckoning. He sat himself down behind the old desk. The hair on his chest curled out of his shirt. It matched the color of his mustache and the hair on his head. Jessie figured him for an old fifty, probably fit and handsome at one time, maybe not very long ago. Town-taming in remote mountains aged a man unfairly. Jessie said she wanted to know what had been done in the investigation of Jessup's disappearance.

"O' course, Miss Starbuck, course— By the by . . ." He ratcheted his wrist in a swigging motion. "Care to join me for a little welcoming drink?"

"No, thanks, but feel free, please."

Nettles nodded and pulled open a drawer.

"Well, ma'am, o' course I examined his cabin real thorough-like. The place was, you might say, a tad disorderly." With a thud, he placed on his desk a tall bottle filled with a sickening red liquid.

"Arvilla told me the place was a shambles," Jessie said, "like there was a fight or— What the hell is *that*?" she asked, wrinkling her nose.

Nettles smiled. "This here's what ya call yer tarantula juice."

"What's in it?"

Nettles chuckled as he poured himself a cupful. "M'own secret recipe, missy. I can tell ya it's coiled down from taters—"

"Distilled?"

"So to say. Damn raw, too. Some folks flavor it with bat guano—if you'll pardon my 'parly vou fran say'—and the red, that come from cinnabar." Seeing Jessie's puzzled look, he added, "Ore o' mercury, missy," and he threw back the entire glass in one gulp. Jessie could hear him swallow,

51

and when his eyes opened, they were tearing. Exhaling, he asked, "Care for a nip?"

Jessie declined with a wince and said, "Arvilla said the cabin was a shambles."

Nettles turned his palms up and looked about his office. "Well, no worse than this place, but if she sez so . . . Anyhow, I did locate a few drops o' blood, doubtful enough to warrant a fight. I had nosebleeds messier than that."

The marshal poured himself another tarantula juice and drawled on about tracing Jessup's trail, this time nursing his drink. The case was further confused, he explained, by the disappearance of Jessup's palomino, too. About a week later, after company hunters found the animal dead at the bottom of a ravine on the far side of the ridge, a search party failed to find Jessup. Word in town was that Jessup was cheating on his assays, was found out, and hightailed it north. Whether he had a mishap or killed the beast to cover his tracks, no one knew. The rumours about Jessup's cheating only carried weight if the people he questioned could be believed: mostly Gore employees—Benton and his cronies.

"One o' them shift bosses says Jessup was a ornery ol' goat, especially when he was on the juice," said Nettles. "Claims Jessup drew some iron on him once, though he disremembers the what-fers perzactly."

This was odd, Nettles confirmed, because, being a drinking man himself, he had invited Jessup to share a spot of the juice many a time and was usually disappointed.

"Not that Orrum never partook, mind you," the marshal affirmed, "but he swore off the stuff 'bout as complete as a drinkin' man could."

Jessie countered by saying, "He may have been a drinker occasionally, Marshal, but Orrum Jessup was not the fighting type, and that cabin of his, there was definitely a fight in that cabin."

"I expect you're right, missy, but it sure would be hard to prove Orrum weren't drunk leastways *some* o' the time—not that I give them dern blatherskites one bit o' creed."

With that, he turned to spit disdainfully into a dented spittoon on the floor behind him. Falling short of his mark, he wiped the mucous string of spittle from his chin with his sleeve.

Clearly there was no evidence that Jessup had tampered with his assays. Nonetheless, Nettles offered to dredge his own reports from his disorderly files, pulling cracker tins, spoons, sharpening stones, and stirrups from the same drawer he thought he had filed them in, mumbling to himself, "So that's where that thang got to!" and "Sombitch don't belong thar." Jessie tried to curtail his useless search repeatedly, until she finally stood up and closed the drawer herself. Standing close to him, she could count the broken blood vessels in his misshapen nose.

She stated that it was obvious there was foul play in Jessup's cabin that night. It would have been easy to make a murder appear to have been a simple disappearance. Evidently Jessup had some enemies, especially among the Gore Company's employees. She insisted there must be something more to be done to find the answers. Nettles's watery eyes were weak. He turned them down. Again he ran his hand across his mouth and nodded.

"I'm terrible scared you're right," he said. "There are things in Redemption no one can know, no one can stop. Jest some things better left unknown."

"That's not good enough, Marshal. I won't settle for that."

"Fact is, Miss Starbuck, if th'ain't no body, ain't no murder."

Back on the street, Jessie took a deep breath as she surveyed this godawful blight of a settlement. She looked through the barred window of Nettles's office to see the sorry lawman pouring another cup of tarantula juice, taller than the others, and getting it down his neck. She drew her shawl tightly around her and headed for the Caribou, feeling sorry for the old coot and somehow excited by the challenge of making something right.

From around the corner of the shoemaker's shop peered a thin man. It was Kyle, and he, too, was excited by the prospect of making something right, but in quite a different way.

At the hotel desk Jessie stopped for her room key and was amused to find a few of Coleson's handbooks there for sale. The image of his sturdy frame, piercing eyes, and enticing smile gave her a bubbly feeling in her chest. She even found herself humming as she ascended the stairs. The feeling stayed with her throughout dinner at the St. Ives, where many of the Cornish miners liked to eat. Her solitary existence these past two weeks was beginning to degenerate into loneliness, and Coleson was easily the most interesting man she had met in some time. Later, from inside her room, she could hear the sound of distant steam engines in the crisp, clear night air. The gulch was relatively quiet, since the stamp mills and smelters had slowed or stopped work till morning. She wished for company.

She stripped down to her petticoat and poured water into the washbowl. It was a far colder wash than she would normally have tolerated, but this was not the Pinnacles. Thankfully, the small stove had been stoked, and the room was almost cozy. Dragging her luggage to the bedside, Jessie sat and rummaged through it, leaving her favorite short riding crop resting across the top. From beneath some denim she lifted out a bundled gunbelt. Within its supple holster of polished cordovan leather was her prized double-action Colt .38, a gift from her father on her eighteenth birthday. It's slate-gray finish always reminded her of the Texas sky she loved. Alex Starbuck had ordered it made specially for her, right down to its peachwood grips. It was a perfect balance between lightweight accuracy and reduced recoil, as it was mounted on a .44 frame.

Putting it aside, she retrieved a pocket diary bound in black leather. Its pages were filled with cryptic scrawls that only she understood. Given to her by her father, the book was not so much a gift as a weapon. In it was a list of names and leads to the various American representatives of the nefarious cabal responsible for her father's murder. Alex Starbuck had compiled the list over many years, revealing its meaning to Jessie only at the point of death, as he confessed to her his lifelong battle and passed it on for her to continue. She had added her own discoveries to the diary along the way. The book was her best informant for identifying enemies of her father and of the nation, and her first weapon in countering their influence. Paging through it in the low lamplight, Jessie was not surprised to find Padgett's name listed in connection with several European industrialists, arms dealers, and bankers, all known threats to America's well-being. She knew that if these unscrupulous snakes went unchecked, the United States wouldn't survive to see its second hundred years.

Returning the diary to her bag, she reclined on the lumpy mattress, putting her bare, shapely legs beneath the covers. As she propped herself on pillows against the brass headrails, her bedsprings creaked until she lay still, her flat, youthful stomach rising and falling with her slowing breath. And yet she heard bedsprings creaking. A gentle knocking became apparent, pricking up Jessie's curious ears. The sounds came from the adjacent room behind her and grew steadily faster and more intense. She could make out the moans of a man and woman, but not their words. They proceeded to buck and bounce in passionate throes.

Feeling secretly sinful and excited, Jessie kneeled close to the wall to hear more despite her embarrassment. Carefully she placed her ear against the wallcloth and covered her other ear as well. It satisfied her not to be able to hear the lovers' exact words—to hear more would have been indecent—but the contours of their mounting, anonymous passion enflamed her loins and made her squeeze her thighs together tightly.

Before long, the lovers' bedsprings were squeaking loudly enough to be heard without an ear pressed to the wall, and the rocking of the bed became a resonant, thudding heartbeat. The cries of pleasure led Jessie to imagine what was happening. She lay back with staring eyes seeing nothing and sensed the warmth in her crotch growing moist. She gave in to wanton fantasy, letting her hands glide over her heaving breasts and stomach, hoping the litany of love next door wouldn't end too soon.

She let her imagination run unbridled, startling herself with its vividness. As her hands wandered down to the mound beneath her white cotton lace, her knees bent slightly, widening her thighs to the imagined presence of the hazel-eyed stranger, John Coleson, kneeling between them. She fantasized that his warm hands were moving up her legs, his muscular chest bare and tanned. She drew one soft shoulder from the petticoat, and imagining her own hand to be that of her dream lover, she freed her luscious breast and teased the pink nipple to erection. With her own saliva upon her fingertips, she moistened the rosy circle surrounding it, pulled and gently twisted it, then grasped the entire breast in one massaging palm.

The momentary lull next door and a more intense resumption of thigh-pounding passion suggested her neighbors had changed position, setting Jessie's imagination afire. In one move, she drew her petticoat to her waist and, pulling it below her round bum, kicked it to the floor. Her fingers combed through her thick, coppery pubic hair, and she lightly palmed her musky vulva while simultaneously stroking her breasts. In her mind, she saw Coleson undoing his belt and opening his pants, releasing his engorged penis to stand at full attention, waiting for her to grasp it, stroke it, suck it.

The intensity of the dream made Jessie writhe. Her toes flexed, and soon her bedsprings, too, voiced their response. Her breathing was deep, and as her head was cast to the edge of the bed, through half-closed eyes she saw the smooth, phallic handle of the riding crop atop her luggage. In a dazed arousal, Jessie snatched it up upon hearing the

56

endlessly repeated cries of hypnotic sensual abandon as the woman next door climaxed and groaned loudly, orgasm upon orgasm.

Dipping two fingers between her enflamed labia, Jessie thrust them into her flowing vagina and drew them out, across her clitoris, drenching it with her juices. While rubbing it up and down, she drew the blunt leather handle of the crop between her breasts and touched it to her sensitive nipples. A flood of warmth swept down her abdomen. She raised one knee high and, reaching around the outside of her thigh, plunged her wet fingers deep into her sex from behind while thrusting the phallic crop down upon her vulva.

Stroking herself from front and back, Jessie fantasized it was Coleson she was pleasing as only a real woman knew how—not as his superior, but as his equal, bringing two halves together as a whole for a brief, godlike moment. Like her father's Japanese housekeeper who had taught her the ways of tantric love with his knowledge and consent— Jessie abandoned herself to the healthy, natural expression of her sexual self as a high art form. Although pleasuring herself, she ached for the touch of a real man, for the chance to please and be pleased. As she pictured in her mind the tall blond stranger grasping the calves of her upraised leg, kneeling to penetrate her, the crop slid easily into her yielding vagina, plunging deep into her belly. Switching hands, she moved the thick staff in and out of her glistening pink pussy while stroking her clitoris side to side with a quick, light touch of her fingers, and as the rocking of the bed next door ceased amid orgasmic grunts, Jessie's body was wracked with erotic spasms as she brought herself to orgasm with the wishful dream of Coleson's spunk ejaculated inside her.

Exhausted, panting, Jessie dropped the crop into her bag. Her hands and inner thighs shone with the purest cum. Curling her naked self like a child beneath her thick blankets, she passed out and slept blissfully to dream of the tall, blond stranger.

★

Chapter 5

Redemption was a town whose saloons seldom slept, but within a short time of Jessie's retiring to her room, the Touchstone was in its peak hours. The bar was lined with muckers elbow-to-elbow, eager to get rid of their company scrip. The card and roulette tables were busily raking in profits for their tenant proprietors—Padgett and Benton among them—except at the faro table, where the geologist John Coleson calmly scrutinized the dealer's deck and consistently won. The air was thick with smoke and swearing. The upright piano against the wall, badly in need of tuning, stood unused. Most of the "Redeemed" had no use for music—unless it was the lubricant for easy sex, and in this mining camp, "easy" usually meant "affordable." But there was one, very desirable woman, a buxom, rosy-cheeked blonde, who almost no one in Redemption could readily afford, and she was as much a fixture at the Touchstone as its brass rails and trophy heads.

Lydia Boudreaux.

Jessie had seen Lydia around the Caribou without taking much heed of her. Striking as she was in some people's eyes, Lydia didn't command attention by virtue of elegance, which she lacked, or intelligence, which was usually a matter of her knowing when to sway her generous hips and for whom. Lydia was the subject of perennial gossip in Redemption, something of an enigma. She dressed in expensive clothing, usually tight-fitting and flattering to her rump and bosom, and was seldom seen unless bound and hung with Hardwick & Knowles's jewelry. She was a long-term guest at the Caribou, where she ate most of her meals, received all her mail, and presumably disappeared to when not at the Touchstone. The largest part of the enigma was how she paid for it all, but that was not the best part.

It was common knowledge that soon after Lydia arrived in Redemption she'd found work as housekeeper and scullery maid for Charles C. Padgett. Commonly known, too, was the story of how Padgett, in a rage that echoed throughout the gulch, had fired the young woman and booted her from his hilltop home. After that, she found what work she could at the Touchstone, as a glorified hurdy-gurdy girl, the most sought-after partner available in the saloon's "Pay As You Dance" offer, which rewarded the lonely mucker with a five-minute dance and a glass of beer or a jolt of tangle-foot for turning over one dollar in gold or scrip to the barkeep. Sometimes an aspiring piano player or drunken prankster was on hand to provide some noise on the ivories.

The best part of the enigma was whose woman she was—beyond the occasional dude every woman in town was expected to bed now and then. Everyone speculated that Padgett must have been her secret paramour; but the reclusive aristocrat was never seen with her, and no one could imagine any woman desiring him.

Virgil Nettles was practically alone in his obsession with Lydia Boudreaux—with her breasts, that is—but he ended more nights spent at the Touchstone asleep on the boardwalk, soaked in his own piss, than he did getting within sniffing range of Lydia. She would often let him buy her drinks, stroking his ego as long as he was paying, and he had never got up the gumption to demand her as a

Pay-As-You-Dance partner. Until tonight.

" 'Scuse me, Miss Lydia," Nettles said, keeping his fin gers proudly tucked in his belt loops. He cleared his throat loudly. "Miss Lydia, I beg your attention."

She was serving drinks to a table, bending low to earn her tips the best way she knew how, while returning the men's change. "Now, you ain't gonna find your coins down there," she sang to one young teamster who got lost in the gorge within her open-necked blouse.

"Miss Lydia," Nettles interrupted, "I do beg your pardon."

Turning to the marshal in exasperation, she said, "Can't you tell I'm ignoring you, Virge? I told you I don't want to dance tonight."

"Go on, Kentucky," said the teamster, using Nettles's most common nickname. "Can't you see you're botherin' the little lady?"

But the old sot was determined. He had put on his cleanest shirt, trimmed with piping, and dusted his boots. He had decided not to call her out on her rude replies anymore; that never got him anywhere. He vowed to be polite. Respectful. Dignified.

"I recollect what you told me, Miss Lydia, but—you spy them two glasses setting on the bar there? One's fer you if you'll be kind enough to join me."

When she accepted and asked his indulgence while she finished serving, Nettles inflated with pride and returned to the bar to await her. His sense of time was badly impaired— it seemed like a dog's age passed and he was thirsting something fierce—so he downed his glass, ordered another, and downed Lydia's before it arrived. When Lydia stood next to him, he was ordering a fourth.

"That one mine?" she asked. She didn't recognize the off-color liquid and, putting the glass to her nose, drew back with a wince. "What in God's country is that?"

Nettles beamed as he held his new glass high. "Taos Lightnin'," he bragged. "My libation o' choice when I can

60

git it. Can't vouch fer its chemistry, but the kick is legend."

"Jeez, Virge, you're gonna hurt yourself someday."

"Ain't nobody made a habit o' this stuff, Lydia—no man ever lived long enough after drinkin' it."

Lydia refused it, so the marshal bought her something she liked. With a tap of their glasses they drank, and then Nettles's hand was on her spine as he professed his long-standing affection for her. She rolled her eyes and fidgeted but didn't want to leave until her glass was emptied. But she was getting fed up. Virgil had been a plague for too long. He offered to leave her alone in exchange for a kiss, as if it were an ultimatum.

"Damn it, Virge, don't you ever quit?"

"Not till you give your marshal a kiss."

"Kiss my ass," she said, spilling her drink as she went off.

"Glad to!"

He sat drinking and mumbling to himself, gesturing with limp hands. Lydia's sneering glances he mistook for proof of her secret desire for him, but if she needed to be discreet, he would respect that. However, the night was getting no younger and his legs no steadier, so he threw down four bits and demanded a dance with no one but Lydia Boudreaux. At first she refused, but the barkeep reluctantly insisted: It was good for business. Besides, Nettles was harmless.

So, without music and before many jeering and whistling onlookers, Virgil and Lydia stepped to the open floor near the center of the room, and the marshal attempted a courteous bow. "Let's get this over with, Virge" was Lydia's curt response, and keeping whatever distance between them possible, she swayed and circled with the smiling old man. She counted the minutes and was wary of Nettles's hand slipping down her back, swearing to herself that if he went too low she'd coldcock him.

"You know how crazed I been fer you, Miss Lydia," he said into her ear. She rolled her eyes. "Don't you get cold and lonely by yerself at night?"

61

"No, Virge, I got my chamber pot close by."

Nettles chuckled. "Aw, Lydia, you always fillin' every ditch I dig. Serious now." He whispered, "Let me have your key so I can mosey up to your room secret-like tonight."

"You got one minute, Virge. Keep dancing."

But Virgil was persistent, and before the full five minutes had elapsed, Lydia pulled away, demanding he "Give it up already." He followed her and drove her to make a decision. Irritated, she said, "All right," and asked him to wait at the bar. When she returned, she wore a warm, inviting smile.

"All right, Virge, you win." She discreetly took his hand and pressed a key into it, saying, "I'll be staying here tonight, the corner room in the back, upstairs. Come around one and be real quiet. Just let yourself in." Virgil leaned over to kiss her, but Lydia shied away. "Not here, Virge. Customers."

At the faro table, the stacks of chips in front of John Coleson had been only a little taller than the carpenter's and much taller than those of a bearded fellow claiming to be an itinerant preacher. The Bible-thumper repeatedly prayed for divine assistance when new bets were placed. He drained his whiskey after each loss, and one of the hurdy-gurdy girls quickly refilled it. He was becoming increasingly riled as more of his chips went from his side of the table to Coleson's.

"The Lord blessed us with recreation," he lectured, "to reward our labors, but there are men in the world who persecute the humble through clever guile—like card counting, for instance."

"I wouldn't make no accusations you can't back up, mister," said the carpenter.

"Simply ruminating about the sad state of the world, brother."

"I ain't your brother," the carpenter mumbled. "Place yer bet."

The dealer turned his cards; the preacher slapped the table. Coleson drew the chips to himself with a smile,

62

remarking that the Lord was smiling upon him. When the preacher insulted whatever god it was watching over the tall blond, Coleson only laughed and asked him to relax. He suggested the preacher leave the game if his streak was in the wrong direction; after all, everyone loses now and then.

The preacher wouldn't hear it. He swore he'd stay in the game until he won his money back. He accused Coleson of wanting him to quit so Coleson could walk off with the winnings unchallenged.

"Suit yourself," Coleson snickered. "I'm sure these other gentlemen would appreciate the chance to help you along in your vow of poverty."

The preacher's denial of any such vow blended with another player's cry, "Hey, look at old Virgil—he got hisself a live one," just as the marshal had begun dancing with Lydia. The faro players all—except for Coleson—turned to watch. He cocked his head and caught sight of the spinning roulette wheel at the next table, a blurred rhythm of color and faceted flashes. He couldn't pull his gaze away. His eyes went suddenly glassy; his smile began to droop. The others didn't notice it right away, but soon his head and hands were trembling. "What the hell—?" began one player as a string of saliva dripped from Coleson's flaccid mouth.

"Hey, mister," said the carpenter. "Mister!" But Coleson couldn't answer.

The preacher slid his chair back, staring with some fright in his eyes. "Lord be . . ."

The carpenter nudged Coleson's shoulder and got no response. He patted him on the back, asking if he was all right, but Coleson's seizure continued. With darting eyes, the preacher said, "The good Lord strikes down sinners and cheaters," and although the carpenter told him to shut up, he continued, "Woe to the card counters." He lurched across the table and swept away a handful of Coleson's chips, but before he could gather them, the click of a gun cocking froze him cold, and he found himself looking down the short octagonal barrel of the carpenter's Remington pocket pistol, its handsome nickel plate glinting in the lamplight.

"Ain't you never heard 'Thou shan't steal,' preacher man?"

Only when the thumper replaced the chips did the carpenter let down the hammer. When Coleson regained his composure and saw his chips disheveled and the carpenter's hand inside his vest, he understood. He wiped his mouth on his sleeve and excused himself gathering his winnings.

To the carpenter he said, "I owe you one, pard," and went to cash in.

The carpenter stared at the others. "You gon' play some cards now?"

Although none of them had ever witnessed a seizure of a petit mal epileptic before and were shaken by it, getting on with the game seemed like the only real issue at hand.

The big-faced clock behind the bar told Marshal Nettles it was one o'clock: time for heaven. He rose to his feet feeling only somewhat unsteady. Could be worse, he mused. He climbed the stairs and walked down the creaking corridor to the back, panting as he neared the corner room. Quietly he slipped the key into the lock and thought he heard movement inside.

"Lydia?" he whispered.

A sleepy "Yes, yes" was the reply, so Virgil turned the key and entered.

"Yes, oh, yes! Harder!"

There before him stood two people, naked but for the woman's black garters and necklaces. She faced a vanity upon which she had one foot, her long slender leg bent high before the mirror. Behind her stood a thin, naked man ramming his thick cock deep into her fleshy pink folds and thick dark hair. Her breasts and buttocks jiggled with each powerful thrust.

The startled man turned. "What the—" he began, withdrawing from the woman. He spun toward Nettles with his shiny erection wagging and hauled off and punched the old

64

marshal right out the door. Nettles hit the opposite wall and slid to the floor. The naked man stood in the doorway ready to hit him again but noticed the marshal's badge peeking out from under his vest. The door slammed shut as he cursed, and there Nettles slept.

Jessie slept so soundly into the cold small hours, it would have taken an explosion to rouse her. And when she awoke with a start in blackness, that was what she imagined she had felt pulsing through the building and into her bed. Going to the window, when she saw lights suddenly dotting the dark mountainsides above town and others appearing down the street, she knew she had felt precisely that. The sickening orange glow of a newborn fire high atop the ridge confirmed it.

The hellish growl from above came to her fluctuating on the wind, rumbling down the hillsides. Within moments, all of Redemption responded. Steam whistles screamed throughout the gulch. People came running from their cabins, pulling on coats and hats, only to find no way to ascend the mountain. Already a small cadre of Padgett's private militia, the Blossom Rock Guard, had commandeered the nearest tramway. Men steered mule-driven disaster equipment crazily up the switchbacks, savagely whipping the snorting sumpters. It was still too dark to see where the trouble was, but after Jessie's useless attempt to snatch more sleep before the reluctant dawn, it was easy to see a column of deadly black smoke billowing from the mouth of the Never Sleep. The morning sun showed that part of the mine's headframe had been blown out sideways.

By the time Jessie was dressed and out of the hotel, the better vantage points for seeing the disaster from the street were already crammed with townspeople standing in the cold with faces upturned. Some women were weeping. Everyone looked scared.

Within two hours, some of the men who had made it out of the shafts alive were arriving in town. With blackened faces and seared lungs, they were herded into the Baptist church. Only a few were injured, but many more were still underground. The account of their escape horrified all who heard them and terrified everyone else who got secondhand, exaggerated retellings. Their piteous stories stunned.

Blasts had occurred in two places nearly simultaneously, though much disagreement surrounded the location of the first one. It was determined that the first crosscut between the Bates and Jump shafts, at the one-hundred-foot level, blew first; the Bates headframe blew next. After escaping a collapsing mine shaft below, some miners perished in the burning Bates shaft house above. Dead were the ones who stayed on to help out the men below. They desperately kept the Westinghouse engines under full heads of steam to keep every cage hoisting survivors; but when the first cage appeared, it was a melted knot of twisted metal enclosing maimed and decapitated bodies. The would-be heroes knew it was futile—and were soon crushed themselves beneath tons of blazing headframe.

Out of the Jump shaft house, which went unscathed, miners in water-soaked clothing streamed down the switchbacks in ore cars and on foot. When the evacuation was complete and no more survivors could be located, a lantern was lowered into the shaft with emergency instructions attached. There was a never a tug. The air blowers were ordered shut, a decision strongly opposed by many. Certain there were still people trapped inside alive, the protesters felt that fresh air was more important than squelching an underground fire no one really knew existed. But in time, the choking black smoke that began to creep from the Jump shaft removed all doubt. Since the Yellow Jacket Mine disaster a little more than ten years earlier, everyone knew a mine fire could burn for weeks. A vibrating sound like distant thunder terminated the most persistent hopes.

Redemption passed the entire day in stunned mourning, but not Charles Calvin Padgett. Having stood in the wagon yard since dawn, bolt upright and with arms folded, his stern expression signaled quiet rage to some, indifference to others. He refused to get any closer to the site and retreated inside the Lodgepole, where he supervised from the window, but more than one miner swore that Padgett didn't care in the least. His superintendent, Ryde Benton, was more agitated, having paced the saloon with clenched fists and knocked back shots of whiskey since before the sun had cleared the ridge. After a huddled talk with his company officers, Padgett stormed off, rudely pushing a miner out of his way, and was driven home. A meeting was announced for the next afternoon in front of the newspaper building.

Jessie figured the crowd in front of *The Telegraph* waiting to hear Padgett speak must account for everyone in the gulch. She stood in the boardwalk across the street for a better view and saw Ki quietly standing among the miners. Coleson appeared, looking somber, and stood near her. People on the fringe of the crowd stared sullenly at the wagon load of coffins lumbering into the wagon yard below.

Padgett was no orator, but he could play a crowd. An alarm bell was beaten before he appeared on *The Telegraph* steps, and then he stood statue-like a while. He recounted the catastrophe, beginning with the assurance that safety was the company's prime concern and there had been no breech of safety precautions. This had been no accident, he insisted; it was sabotage. Mass murder. Eleven had been killed, two of them dying overnight of their injuries. He promised support to the families. And vengeance—along legal channels. There was evidence, he said, that one of their most unscrupulous competitors, Grand River Mining under the insidious direction of Jefferson D. Atwood, was at the root of the atrocity, and he called upon the governor to step in. Being certain to include a reference to the Never Sleep's promising new finds, Padgett bewailed the loss of life and material.

Without taking his eyes off Padgett, Coleson said, "The man sure shuffles a stacked hand."

The Gore Company president publicly condemned violence while laying responsibility for the crime upon Atwood, and called upon the Grand River Mining owner to defend himself on record. His speech did little more than inflame the townspeople, not only toward Atwood, but toward the Gore Company, as well. The disaster made the miners reluctant to return underground, and those who didn't show for their shifts found themselves without jobs. The Lodgepole was such a hotbed of bad temper, the Blossom Rock Guard was called in to maintain order.

Nightfall found Ryde Benton sitting at his regular table in the Touchstone, sounding out words from a newspaper Padgett had given him earlier. The headlines and firsthand accounts were garish, unbelievable. His reading was so slow, he tired of it soon and leafed through, looking at the etchings. An undertaker's advertisement in the back showed an open coffin with a plush interior. He sounded out the words: "No delay. I promise to keep a full line of coffins and caskets in stock . . . I have a new corpse preserver." He thought the word "corpse" was French.

Through the window, he saw the tall figure of a man carrying a heavy satchel, coming off the trail from the mines. As the man crossed the yard, Benton saw he had blond hair beneath his brown wide-brimmed hat—the guy Kyle had told him about. He remembered seeing Coleson around town—never wearing trousers as dirty as they were now—and he was fairly certain Coleson didn't do anything for the company.

Taking Kyle along, Benton followed the tall stranger at a distance, up Eagle Road to the marshal's office. They watched him go in. Benton didn't like that. He sent Kyle back to the Touchstone for some help while he stayed on. It was a good half hour before Coleson emerged again, and this time there were four people watching.

Walking back down Eagle on his way home, Coleson disliked the stance of a man stepping into the path ahead of him, so he decided on a shortcut through an alley. When he had come about halfway through, two silhouetted figures, one of them enormous, appeared at the other end. He looked back. The first man he had seen was joining another in blocking the rear escape. He cursed beneath his breath. His only choice was to force an exit the way he had come in. He rushed the two men in a sudden turn, fishing one hand into his satchel as he went.

"I wouldn't try it!" shouted Benton as he and Kyle moved into the alley from the far end.

★

Chapter 6

Coleson didn't reveal his hand until he was within striking distance. The first man bit the dust when a surprise side-arm wallop with Coleson's two-pound maul opened a serious gash in the side of his head. The second man rushed him just before Benton and Kyle reached them. Coleson kept moving forward with one elbow raised, nailing the second man square in the windpipe. He followed through with an upward swing of the maul, driving the top of the head into the rogue's ribs and putting him down. Then Benton's huge hands clamped down upon his shoulders.

In a heap they fell to the ground, Coleson right in the middle, and Benton somersaulted over him. Coleson kept himself rolling, dropping his bag and circling around with his elbow, finding Benton's jaw between it and the earth. At the same time, Kyle pounced, flailing his fists at Coleson's face and chest. The tall blond hit him twice in the side with the heavy steel maul and, when his other hand came free, pistoned his square fist right into Kyle's grimacing face and catapulted him back. Kicking the third man off his legs in a frenzy of adrenaline, Coleson scrambled to his feet and tried to run for it, but Benton tripped him and clawed at his trousers. He got to his feet again just as the third man reached him, and before he could get up to speed, he was tackled and hit the ground chest-first, getting the wind knocked out of him.

Two men raised him to his knees. Coleson wrapped his arms around them, holding on. He couldn't breathe. He heard Benton say, "You ain't gonna show your face near them mines or near that marshal ever again." His drooping head was suddenly slammed back to his spine by the pulverizing crash of Benton's anvil fist, sending a spray of saliva skyward. "You shittin' mama's boy," Benton whispered, "you best stay on at home." Another fist thrusted into his stomach like a ramrod, doubling him over. "Mind your damn business." Coleson looped one bent leg around as many legs as he saw beside him and, leveraging himself by the shoulders, tripped them over to one side before Benton could land his next blow.

One man fell on top of him, painfully twisting his arm that got tangled in the clothing. Not finding an escape, he instead found himself on his knees once more, this time to receive a devastating kick to the head by Benton. He had closed a bloody eye as Benton's boot drew back for another when a gunshot exploded with a lightning flash and a cloud of dirt kicked up at their feet. The fighters leapt. Coleson fell to the ground, barely able to see the shadowed figure of a girl holding her Colt with both hands, aiming at Benton.

"Get off him *now*!"

Before the dust cleared, Kyle kicked Coleson in the ribs and another deafening discharge scared them back. Jessie rushed up, stuck the barrel of her revolver right in Kyle's face, hissing curses at him, then smashed him hard in the jaw with it. As he hit the dirt, she spun and targeted Benton to prevent another attack.

"I swear I'll not hesitate killing all of you, and I know I can!" she warned.

Benton and his boys put their palms up and jeered the "little girl with the big gun" in calm voices. They backed off some before, feeling comfortable enough to turn their backs on her, glancing over their shoulders as they left. While the other two helped their wounded friend, Benton walked off pointing at her. "Now, don't you get mixed up with mama's boy trash like that. Y'hear?"

Helping Coleson to his feet, Jessie asked, "You badly hurt?" The cut over his eye didn't look terrible, but he'd be knots in the morning. "I told you we'd be crossing paths again soon."

Coleson was the type who'd never let hurt pride get in the way of being a gentleman. Especially to a lady. "Thank y', Miss Starbuck." He leaned against the building, clutching his gut. His face was wry with pain. "Thanks much."

"Call me Jessie."

His eyes opened suddenly, in disbelief.

"I liked that name the first time you said it."

Jessie smirked. "Thrilling. Suddenly you don't seem so hurt. Where do you live?"

Coleson clutched his gut harder and insisted he could make it home alone, didn't want to put her out. All he needed was to catch his breath and his belongings. His explanation for the assault sounded routine—just another bad mix of money, cards, and booze. Jessie doubted that; those thugs would have been more persistent if money were at stake. The ambush had the smell of terror. She walked with him a ways. Coleson was gallant, offering to escort her, but the Caribou was just ahead.

"You should be careful round here at night," Jessie advised. She put a friendly hand on his arm. Coleson caught himself staring at her as she entered the Caribou.

He walked off, scrutinizing every alley he passed. Turning into a dark street, he rummaged through his jacket. He withdrew a wallet, paused, and looked through it. He removed a wad of paper currency and some scrip, closed the wallet, and chucked it into a rain barrel. Another wallet came from inside his pants. Again he searched for what he could use, then drowned it in the barrel. From beneath his armpits came a small leather pouch. There he hit paydirt—two gold nuggets, some dust, and some coins. *Plop!* into the barrel with the deflated bag, and off he went. He thought, At least they paid for the pleasure of rolling me.

Virgil Nettles, keeper of law and order in Redemption, was oblivious to Coleson's run-in with Benton. He never saw Benton leave the Touchstone because at the time his eyes were fixed on Lydia Boudreaux entering the saloon. She wasn't wearing her working clothes. From his seat at the end of the bar, Nettles could see her before she noticed him and was fired up to scold her. He was instead surprised that, when she spotted him, she hurried to him with apologies. She put a warm, smooth hand to his bruised cheekbone and pursed her lips when she spoke.

"Honest, Virge, I didn't know it was the wrong key. I just wasn't looking at which one I took. Please, let me make it up to you."

It took a couple more minutes than Lydia had anticipated, but she soon had Nettles apologizing for his own poor behavior and asking to make things up to her. With a flourish of her hand, she got the bartender to serve up two drinks, and Lydia's curvaceous body brushed so close to Nettles's legs, the satin of her dress hissed across his denim. She confessed to being rude to the old marshal; after all, she knew how hard life had been on him, he being a widower and such. Her brow knit in deepest empathy.

"Truly, I feel terrible," she assured him. Every time her hand returned from placing her glass on the bar, she let it brush across Nettles's thighs, closer to his crotch each time. She squeezed his hand suggestively after telling him she had the night off and wouldn't mind sharing a few drinks with him—if he wasn't too angry with her. He snorted in embarrassment. He wasn't as drunk as he had been the night before.

"I really like you, Virge," she said, staring him in the eye. "Really."

73

Small talk flowed along with another drink for the marshal—the explosion, the lock-in. What a pity about the Never Sleep. The victims, too. Every once in a while Lydia would make casual references to her living alone. Working at night. The loneliness. What a pity. Or else she'd confess to some measure of guilt over his bruise, and she had to keep her mind straight about just what she was saying. She asked him what he could possibly see in her, a nobody. Here he was, Virgil Nettles, Town Marshal of Redemption, an able-bodied, available man who could have his pick of the ladies.

"Just yesterday I saw you eyeing that pretty strawberry blonde in your office," she taunted.

That's when Nettles blurted Jessie's name. He assured her Jessie's visit was purely business, and Lydia sidestepped, saying, "Why ever you'd choose me over her I never—"

As with a circling hawk, every swoop Lydia made in the conversation toward Jessie came closer than the one before. She didn't really know what she needed to know about her, and she sure wasn't learning anything new, though she prodded often and listened hard. Nettles had only Lydia on his mind.

She shot her eyes toward the door in the back and took Nettles's hand. "Come along, Virge, I'm gonna make it up to you right now."

Her smile disappeared as soon as she turned away. She led him through the door, Nettles in tow whispering, "Whar in tarnation you takin' me to?" and giggling. Across from the rear door she backed into a shallow closet, pulling the marshal in with her. She swallowed and took a deep breath as she ran her hands down the marshal's trousers. She pressed her large breasts against his chest to make them bulge upward and show her cleavage. With one finger she pulled her bodice down over one breast, barely revealing a blush brown oval to Nettles before covering it up. She whispered, "It wants you, Virge." Stroking the lawman's crotch, Lydia worked him up into a heavy-breathing dither that made him rock his hips. She embarrassed him when she moaned, so she grabbed his backside and moaned more softly. He forgot his pride.

She grinded her pubic mound against his erection, which was difficult because of his large gut. When his breathing became a pant, she knew the time had come to unbutton his pants, one by one. Lowering herself to her knees, her face against his stomach, she touched his penis and withdrew it, then stood up and proceeded to bemoan the fact that he was receiving visits from another woman, unmarried and younger than herself.

In Nettles's zealous mind, he needed a smooth defense, and what she said about Jessie didn't matter; getting Lydia to continue did. And while Lydia wasn't up on everything going on in Redemption, the town was small; so when Nettled dropped Arvilla Jessup's name to explain Jessie's visit, Lydia made a note to remember. Flattered, Nettles denied any involvement with the beautiful Texan.

"I swear, Miss Lydia, compared to you, Miss Starbuck's all vine and no taters."

Lydia knew what she had to do, and what she couldn't do, which was run away. She mustered her courage and, breathing slowly to relax her gag reflex, dropped to her knees again to make up to Virgil the beating she had won him the night before.

One hour past sunup, Ki and a wagonload of miners were taking a journey ride up the steep Valhalla Trail. They were among the daily wagon train of men and equipment that had to be dragged up more than a thousand vertical feet along two miles of treeless switchbacks to the small satellite camp that worked the Valhalla and Witless mines, the Gore Company's two best silver producers. Ever since rising, he hadn't been able to shake the fact that he'd be replacing one of the eleven killed in yesterday's sabotage, a dubious honor that still paid the three-and-a-half dollars a day the dead men had earned—"Far below standard," according to

75

Pender, the long-winded old-timer who shared Ki's room. But then, everything was below standard for these miners, as far as Ki could see. His "room"—his gopher hole—which was no more than a log-walled burrow in the side of the mountain and roofed with canvas, wasn't fit for the possums that scurried through at night. Pender, who had "seen it all" and wasn't afraid to tell it, told of brutal winters with snow that fell gray in Marmot Gulch.

The sight that finally shut Pender's mouth was two buckboards loaded with coffins lumbering up a distant trail toward the Never Sleep, where searches were in full sway. But he was too cynical to stay silent long, and most everything Pender said piqued Ki's curiosity.

"They allus bringing them boxes round, not just today. They come up here heavier than when they leave."

Pender had been appointed Ki's mucking partner by the pit foreman, Boyd. About all a mucker needed to know was how to load ore cars with rock that was hot enough to scald, and stay out of the way. "Dyin's the easy part," Pender said. "The pit takes care of everything else," with burning floods, cave-ins, bad-air, explosive gases . . . No wonder they call it "the pit," Ki thought.

At the top of the rise, the rusting metal sides and roof of the towering shaft house came into better view. It enclosed the mine shaft headframe with odd-angled eccentricity. The operation at this altitude was at various stages of development, Ki judged, seeing a few mule-driven hoists. As the arriving miners gathered outside the building, several Blossom Rock Guardsmen, armed to the teeth, supervised the body search of each man leaving the mines for the day.

"It's said, ore's so rich here," Pender told Ki, "they send it way the hell to the Brits fer to be milled. Reckon it's bringing better'n a thousand to the ton, and thar's more to be had. But I'll tell ya, it don't look like no high grade I ever seed."

At the signal of a guard, the new shift workers filed through the door beneath the large plaque marked "Witless."

Within the vast emptiness of the building was an intricate skeleton of wood and metal laced with pipes and cables and beams and pulleys. The noise of the steam engines barely let Ki hear his own thoughts, much less the orders barked by the guards. They herded the men through great square-set beams to where three cages hung, two for hoisting men and material. Candles mounted high on the cage shed pale light over their heads. When a dozen men were crowded into the cage, a deafening steam whistle roared. Ki watched while tons of block ice were loaded to be used for drinking water and as protection against the infernal heat at the extreme depths.

With a downward jerk, the cage started its descent.

The moment the irregular rock walls surrounded them, candles and lamps seemed inadequate. Hot air rushed up through the cage. Continuously the rock swept by, suffocatingly, endlessly black, for more minutes than Ki could count. Shadows danced from below, then light appeared, then shadows from above as the cage moved past a square-timbered stope at the one-hundred-foot level. Down they fell—one hundred fifty, two hundred feet—amid echoing squeaks of machinery and faint, distant rumbling.

When at last the cage came to a bouncing stop at the two-hundred-fifty-foot level, Ki stared down an arrow-straight drift as far as his eyes could see, lit with a sky's worth of starlike candles in holders pinned into the rock walls and casting eerie shadows all about. There must be thousands of candles in this tunnel alone, Ki figured. Their odd, blue-green light shone off the silvery rails, over which stood little mules and rough-coated horses with candles on their collars, waiting to haul the small wooden ore cars. The animals' tails and legs were stained a bright green—salt and copper sulfite, Pender explained—to make them more visible. Many of the critters never knew daylight their entire lives. A "red wagon" fitted with an outhouse seat on top and stinking badly stood in a niche on a rail pull-out. The rock walls were too hot to touch.

"Makes you wonder if we ain't diggin' fer hell, ay?" Pender said with a wink. Ki remarked about the narrowness of the tunnel, and Pender replied, "Ain't room enough to cuss a cat and not gettin' a mouthful o' fur."

With Pender's guidance, Ki took his place with other muckers in the square-set tunnel, doing the back-breaking work of loading the ore cars. When a drift was cleared of ore, holes were cut into the wall for the next drift round, a precisely spaced series of explosives that would bring down another layer of ore and advance the tunnel. Although a tunnel was cleared of men for such detonations, it felt and sounded to Ki as if the entire mountain were about to fall in on them.

A solid hour of grueling work elapsed. Standing with yet another armful of ore, Ki was chilled to see the scrawny shift boss, Kyle, standing alongside the ore car. Ki didn't like the smile he was wearing.

"Okay, Hop Sing, I need you fer another job down thisaways," he called.

"I am not Chinese," Ki answered seriously.

"I don't give a good goddamn what the hell y'are, now git yer ass movin'."

He led Ki down the rails to a winze, a vertical shaft connecting two horizontal tunnels, where they boarded a small cage and were lowered to another level.

"You done some double-jackin', Chinaman?" Kyle pried. "Huh? You know how to hold a cold chisel?" Ki affirmed he did, trying to remain calm, but as they exited the winze, Kyle described plans that made Ki nervous.

"I got you the jacking pardner of yer life," Kyle taunted, "and I think you two will get along right neighborly. Name's Big Dave the Dog-eater." His laugh sounded like a cough. At a turn into a small stope, he stopped and faced Ki. "And I'll tell you right up, Chinaman, you don't wanna cross Big Dave." Behind him worked the foul-smelling brute who was among the last to see Orrum Jessup alive.

78

"This here's Big Dave the Dog-eater," Kyle said. He folded his arms and gloated. "This man could make a meal out'n a keg o' ten-penny nails, easy. Rumor has it ol' Dave done et two live wolfhounds, one fancy show dog, and a missionary. I reckon you two might get real friendly-like." He started to walk away, then turned and said, "Oh, by the by, Big Dave's got a real mean nerve toward you Chinamen, considering how dirty y'all are." His eyes sparkled.

Without warning, Big Dave chucked a steel chisel nearly two feet long at Ki, who easily caught it in one hand. The bad-smelling Dog-eater stared closely at the folds of Ki's eyes. He tilted his head to indicate where Ki was to place the chisel and lifted a long-handled six-pound sledge to his shoulder. Passing to one side of the man, Ki winced at the man's dunglike body odor. He knelt beside a low ledge of rock, and, keeping his eyes locked on Dave's, placed the chisel and held it tightly with both hands at arm's length.

Big Dave adjusted his grip, inhaled, and swung with a wheeze. The mallet bounced squarely off the chisel head with a *ting*, sending a piercing jolt through Ki's arms. Dave's bulging eyes were arrogant. Again he swung, again the sledgehammer bounced. A wider, much slower swing arced forward, came down, and with no clear *ting*, glanced off the edge of the head, the flailing hammer swiping Ki's sleeve. Big Dave leaned over with confidence to inspect the chisel, dusting it with his breath. Ki's face wilted at the stench.

"Problem, Chink?"

"You smell so bad you could knock a fly off a turd. And I'm not Chinese."

Dave just stood ready with his hammer. "Set it up, Chink."

Ki inhaled audibly and focused on his grip. Now he looked straight ahead, taking in the entire peripheral scene. He saw the big man drawing the mallet well enough to

79

see his face twitch with the strain of the swing. He perceived the subtle shift in Dave's stance as the mallet arced, and how differently his forearm muscles rippled from the way they had in previous swings. In the split second it took for Big Dave to strike, Ki dropped one arm and the plummeting sledge pulverized the gravel below where his wrist had been.

At the end of Dave's grunt, Ki quietly said, "If I thought it was possible to beat that carcass-stink off you, I'd do it gladly."

"All tongue and no gut!" Dave roared as he lunged, thrusting the hammer handle at Ki's throat, but Ki's *age-uki* forearm block deflected it and started Big Dave on a forward tumble to Ki's side.

What ensued during the following two minutes was the most remarkable humiliation any old-timer could recall. In this one man, a son of two cultures and accepted by none, the time-honored way of the warrior, *budo*, had been honed to the keenest, hardest sword edge, for Ki was as committed to the honorable confrontation of two equally equipped forces as he was incapable of admitting defeat. Using common tools as weapons seemed like a mere *kobudo* drill here in the tool-littered tunnel. At every turn he met Big Dave's thundering onslaught, equaling what he didn't foil, taking up a shovel, chisel, or pick only to disarm his opponent. The shadowy cave echoed with Ki's repeated spirit yells, which drew upon the limitless *chi* that powered him. A final series of three high-sweeping, circular kicks to Big Dave's face stunned him stupid and mingled blood and saliva at the corner of his mouth. Kyle had witnessed everything since he heard Dave's first guffaw and now stood in awe of the victorious mucker before him. He feared Ki, maybe desperately. But his mind was squirming with ideas for owning him. He knew one thing in an instant: From that moment forward, he had to treat Ki as a friend.

★

Chapter 7

Charles Calvin Padgett seldom left his home, yet was never on time joining his guests for dinner. He found most conversation unpleasant and most eating a chore, so the less time spent on either, the better. He did like his drink—heavy ports, cognacs, and brandies—so as soon as he lit upon his chair at the head of the table where Ryde Benton and Lydia Boudreaux sat, he was already holding his wineglass out demandingly for his manservant to fill it. He said little to his guests, spread his silk napkin on his lap, and commenced eating. Lydia intently observed Padgett's obsessive habits of wiping his silverware clean before using it and touching his napkin to his mouth after nearly every mouthful. He made her nervous, whereas Benton barely paused in his feeding frenzy.

Thinking himself a gentleman, Padgett toasted Lydia's beauty and complimented her typically low-cut satin evening dress. Her gap-toothed smile was wide, almost bashful, but her eyes sparkled with lust when she touched Padgett's hand.

"So, tell me, Lydia, did we have a profitable evening yesterday?" he asked.

Lydia played with the food on her gold-trimmed china plate and said that Nettles had had little to say to her, try as she might to get him talking. The memory of the episode in the closet was unwelcome, but she was proud she had one small nugget of value to give.

"You were right, C.C. That Starbuck girl is cavortin' about with that Arvilla Jessup."

"And that means Atwood, too," he added.

Benton said, "Atwood ain't nothing to fret, is he? He's a judge—too honest and stupid."

Irritated, Padgett snapped, "The stupid one around here, Ryde, is the one who rode eight hours in the wrong direction looking for the Talisman lode!" More calmly he added, "The only honest judge is one who, once he's bought, stays bought. Period. Everyone else would happily stab me in the back. Lydia, did the marshal tell you what Starbuck's after?"

"Not really, but—"

"No 'not reallies' and no 'buts'! I send you out to do something that would help *me* out for a change—remember *me*?—and all I get is 'not really'?"

" . . . But I'm pretty sure it was about Miss Jessup's father. I recollect he said so, C.C."

Padgett seemed happier with that. He even commended her "expert sleuthing" and promised her a very special reward.

"Isn't she a beauty?" he asked Benton. "She has the body of a goddess and the mind of a playful child. Don't you, my dear?"

She feigned embarrassment, dropping her face, then looked up at Padgett through the tops of her seductive, painted eyes. She squirmed a little on her seat as Lance cleared the table.

When the manservant reappeared, he set before them small finger bowls filled with steaming water. Lydia awkwardly followed Padgett's lead as he squeezed half a lemon into the water, bathed his fingers, and wiped them on

82

his napkin. Benton left his bowl unused. They rose and drifted into the parlor, where Lance had more drinks waiting for them.

Benton remarked that Jessie could be troublesome, judging by his run-in with her during Coleson's ambush. Padgett agreed, but dismissed Coleson as nothing more than an additional nuisance, easily dealt with.

"Yeah," Benton said, "maybe this new guy Kyle told me about could be good. Kyle says he's tough as a pine knot."

Benton's description of the tall, Asian-eyed stranger struck Padgett like a ringing bell. He recognized the description of Ki, Jessica Starbuck's Japanese-American bodyguard. The Starbuck empire extended throughout the mining regions of the West, and Starbuck assay offices were scattered from Cheyenne to Taos. His mind percolated with ideas for foiling whatever it was the meddlesome Miss Starbuck was planning.

"Lydia, darling," he cooed, nuzzling closer to her, "I may have one more little errand for you, a harmless little favor to me."

Lydia hated Padgett's "little favors," but felt she had no choice. "If it makes you happy, C.C." was her usual reply.

"What an incredible specimen you are," Padgett hummed, the alcohol thick on his breath. The hand he had on her thigh rose deliberately to her breast, and Lydia gently tried to resist, feeling simultaneously unsure with Benton in the room and uninhibited by the strong drink she had consumed. Padgett stood and, taking Lydia's hand, led her out of the room. They passed Lance in the hallway.

"Bring some cognac to my room," he said and threw a glance back at Benton before climbing the staircase.

He sat Lydia alone on his high bed and retreated to his wardrobe, emerging a few minutes later dressed in a rich-colored silk robe and loose-fitting pants. Lance was just decanting the cognac into two crystal glasses. Handing one to Lydia, Padgett toasted her beauty once again. The already tipsy blonde sipped it, then, at Padgett's goading, drank down the entire glass. He set down the glasses and stood close to her, roughly thrusting his cold hands down her dress to fondle her ample bosom. He became entangled in his groping, and Lydia felt guilty and ungrateful for her feelings of revulsion. As Padgett pulled and tore at her clothing, she reluctantly helped him remove them, unaware of the door quietly opening and closing and the big man now standing in the corner.

Soon Lydia was half-stripped, her corset and garters tangled around her waist. Padgett leaned over her, harshly kneading her delicate flesh, pinching her nipples until they hurt and rubbing her vulva bearishly. All the while she stroked his groin and wrapped her feet around his waist. He bent closer and whispered hotly in her ear, telling her this was her special reward for being so clever, so useful, so sexy. His language became foul, as it did in no other situation, and he spread her legs wide to view her.

"I have a special reward for us both, my dear," he said and moved to one side. Before her stood a naked Ryde Benton, his eyes fixed on her pubis as he stroked himself to erection.

Unable to say no, Lydia only whimpered, "Please, C.C., it's *you* I want, please," but Padgett didn't hear. He kissed her sloppily and licked her face. He brushed her pubic hair, then swept up her leg and spread her wide as Benton entered her. Padgett continued to kiss and nibble her face as Benton's lunges became powerful, regular thrusts; then he stepped back and sat in an armless chair beside his cognac to watch. Lydia's eyes remained shut throughout most of the ordeal, but she glimpsed Padgett fondling himself with the monogrammed silk damask enshrouding his erection. Then Benton maneuvered her onto her knees, and before she shut her eyes again, she saw Padgett working himself into a stifled frenzy.

It was done. Benton dressed and left the room. Padgett wrapped his flaccid penis in the silk cloth and closed his pants over it. Lydia sat up and tried to fix her hair. Pulling part of her dress around her, she came to kneel meekly between Padgett's legs.

"Was that all right for you, C.C.? Hmmm?" His breathing was still heavy as she began stroking his crotch. "I wish you would do that to me—I mean I liked it—but I want you," she purred.

"I've got one more tiny favor to ask of you, my dear," Padgett said, ringing a small bell on the serving tray, "and I think you'll like this one even better."

Lydia understood this in a way Padgett hadn't meant it. She opened his trousers, and, removing the silk surrounding his cock, she leaned down to take him in her mouth. Padgett smacked her across the face so hard she fell back on the floor with a cry.

"Don't you try your whorin' shit with me. I'll tell you what to do," he growled.

As Lydia begged not to be hit again, gasping apologies and struggling to her feet, Lance knocked on the door. Padgett told her to gather her things as he opened it. Then he rushed her out, giving her no time to dress, saying he would tell her what he needed shortly and to wait downstairs. While she stood outside, eyes tearing and makeup smeared, Padgett said, "That's all for now," and swung the door to enclose himself and his handsome manservant in the privacy of his bedroom.

That very night at the Atwood ranch, Arvilla was wrenched, screaming, from a deep sleep by what sounded like a cannon blast. The shuttered window near her bed exploded in a shower of splintered wood and glass, and the wooden crucifix on the opposite wall disintegrated when the buckshot hit. She threw herself in her quilt to the floor and rolled under the bed in time for a minute-long barrage of small-arms fire into her room.

"Arvilla!" Judge Atwood shouted from down the hall. "You all right?"

"Yes!" she yelled when, as fast as it had started, the gunfire ceased. With her chin to the floor, Arvilla could hear the crackling echo through the valley with the receding sound of hooves. Unable to see anything from her window, she spun on her heels and angrily kicked a chair over.

Arvilla couldn't tolerate the feeling of being hog-tied, and that's what this was like. The only way for her to be rid of it was to put some fire underneath some people's asses, namely Marshal Virge Nettles's. So by noon next day, she trotted her buckboard into Redemption to find Jessie, their next stop being the marshal's office.

Nettles was cold sober when they arrived. It looked to Jessie as if he hadn't even had an eye-opener. Arvilla feverishly recounted what had happened, but when she demanded Nettles come out of the ranch to provide protection, Nettles opened his overstuffed file cabinet and withdrew a flask of Old Overholt. Hc slugged down a burning throatful and avoided the ladies' judgmental eyes.

"Marshal," Jessie intervened, "you are the law here. If you ain't going to do something about this, the least you could do is bring in some help. You've got to call in the county."

Nettles raised the flask for another swallow, but Jessie stopped his wrist.

"Marshal," she said, "please. What are you going to do?"

Practically whispering, he said, "I'm gonna be buried in the sump of some old paid-out mine shaft, you keep rilin' these godawful sumbitches round here. You got it into yer pretty little head you gonna muddy up some folks' creeks, but you don't got the least notion o' what yer steppin' in. And you come in here with this persnickety Miss Jess—"

Arvilla's swift kick to his shins shut him up fast, and she harangued him with insult and venom while Jessie fought back a grin. But after Arvilla had spent her odium and walloped the limping marshal across his head with an open hand, Jessie had more compassion for her, whose predicament left the feisty lass in tears as soon as they were outside.

"I'm scared," Arvilla sobbed. "They're gonna come back. I know it."

Jessie took her by the shoulders and said, "C'mon, let's get my things from the hotel. We're going to telegraph Fort Steele—I have a good friend up there—then I'm coming out there with you."

A moonless, overcast night drew over the Atwood spread like a blanket, going from day to night without twilight. A disquieting stillness clung to the earth. From a distance, the lazy spiral of smoke coming from the ranch house seemed frozen, and one by one, lamps were doused and windows shuttered. By ten o'clock the stillness was unbroken . . . except for a short column of shadowy horsemen cresting a hill near the valley's edge.

The front of the ranch house faced south, toward the mouth of the valley, and with adjoining stables aligned east and west, the compound formed a long L that encompassed a corral. A pair of bays there became skittish as the quiet intruders approached. One horse's neighing was all that broke the silence before gunfire erupted on three sides of the house.

To the invaders' utter amazement, however, their gunfire was returned from two upstairs windows, nearly putting their mounts to flight right out from under them. Whooping and howling like Indians, the raiders circled the building, firing on the gallop into any window they could hit, not realizing that their surprise had been anticipated and no targets were there.

Inside, Jessie and Arvilla knelt behind furniture placed against their bedroom windows to protect their heads as they aimed. Arvilla steadily levered new rounds into the judge's Winchester '73, aiming and firing with care until she had exhausted its fifteen rounds and the octagonal barrel was searingly hot. At her knee lay a box of .44–40s and Atwood's single-action Colt Army. "Load!" she shouted, passing the rifle to the judge crouching behind her. She snatched up the Colt and resumed firing until the judge returned the rifle and began loading the interchangeable ammo into the pistol.

At the other window, Jessie squeezed round after round from her double-action .38. She kept by her side as back-up the judge's prized "Big Fifty," the massive Sharps .50-caliber breechloader given to him by a former buffalo runner. Jessie preferred reloading her Colt to tiring herself under the weight of the Sharps. Through the racket of gun-fire, she heard Arvilla call out, "They're moving behind us! I'm going downstairs," and she saw the girl and the judge crouching toward the stairs.

Scrambling across the sitting room floor on all fours, Arvilla slid to a small window beside the chimney, punched the barrel of her pistol through the glass, and commenced firing. She slid the spent weapon back toward the judge, who slid the Winchester to her in return, but by then the riders had again shifted toward the front to worry Jessie upstairs.

Arvilla lunged for a front window, smashing another pane. From the right, she followed a rider sweeping across and, giving the shot just enough lead, fired. Because of the way he dropped the reigns and his weapon, she was certain she had hit him in the arm, but he didn't fall. She jumped with fright as another rider rumbled across the wood porch just inches in front of her face. She reacted to fire, but the window burst asunder as something heavy crashed into the room. Arvilla fell to the floor and slid behind an armchair, her face dotted with bloody pinpricks. The clopping of hooves faded, and Arvilla stared at an oblong parcel wrapped in brown paper lying beneath a table.

Jessie came down, checking damages. Rosilda and her son emerged from an inner room unharmed. When Jessie saw Arvilla sliding the package toward her, she reacted.

"Is there a fuse? Nothing burning?"

"No," Arvilla said.

Jessie picked it up and shook it. Turned it over. It looked wet. Atwood came forward with a knife and proceeded to cut it open. When the last flap of soggy paper had been lifted away, Arvilla let out a dreadful screech and leapt, scratching and clawing, away from the hideous contents, which had reduced her to a helpless, weeping child. Jessie recognized the dried and blackened mass as the severed four-fingered hand of Arvilla's father.

★

Chapter 8

The Touchstone was more mellow than usual that night, Benton and some of his colorful crew being elsewhere. Lydia was pleased to see the tall stranger called Ki sitting alone, his back to a wall. She could tell he was no real miner, not for any length of time, at least. He was too clean, unscarred, unbeaten. Too handsome. Maybe Padgett was right: She could like this job better.

Approaching a miner didn't take much savvy, so Lydia was good at it. Her best assets were always in plain sight. First the eye contact, a shy smile. Next she sauntered over to his table, drink in hand, and asked to join him. Of course, Ki accepted; after all, he had seen hell in the form of the Witless.

She was calm. She didn't struggle to make embarrassing talk, but admitted wanting someone to talk to, the night being so slow. If he didn't want to talk, she said, she'd understand and leave. She surprised him.

Ki didn't expect to be picked up by anyone in Redemption. Her need for conversation seemed authentic. And she was undeniably sexy, right down to the way her mouth

creased when she smiled. Lydia, too, had green eyes, like
Jessie.

They drank and talked quietly. She told him she worked
there at the Touchstone some nights. Ki easily created an
entire life's fiction for himself, assuming the role he created
so easily even he came to believe it for stretches of time.
And although he knew Lydia survived by her smile, he
wasn't positive she didn't mean it when she called him
"Different. And attractive."

They talked and drank; they grew to like each other.
Banter became a trade, sexual innuendo their stock. But
after nearly an hour and a half, with Ki becoming more
interested in her luscious charms, Lydia saw the big clock
and put down her glass.

Placing a warm hand on Ki's, she said, "I'm so sorry.
It may not be proper for me to stay much longer—though
I'm so glad we met." She stood and reluctantly removed
her hand. "I would love to talk and talk."

Disappointed, Ki resisted appearing so. He pronounced
the clock too fast, but couldn't seem to dissuade her.

"I must walk you to your door then," he said.

They walked out slowly together. Lydia often paused to
look into Ki's quiet eyes. As they cornered the Touchstone,
she stopped.

"Ki, I must tell you something. Please don't think bad
of me. I didn't really have to leave just now. I could have
stayed and talked, but . . . the truth is, I needed to get out of
there. I really wanted to talk to you without all those eyes
on us. I want to tell you something."

She took a deep breath.

"You must realize that I'm no saint. There's not a woman—or a man—in Redemption who is. But I don't want
you to think I go around saying this to different men every
night. I don't. You can see I work here. The guys all respect
me. They know I'm not like . . . one of those girls. I don't
know how to say this except . . . I'm real attracted to you,
stronger than I can tell. It's been so long since I've come

across a real human being. I mean, look at this town! You know how hard it is to find someone like you? Someone normal? I've been here a long time, and you . . . It doesn't get much better, and I won't settle for less when it does.

"I guess what I'm saying is, I'd like to spend some time with you."

Ki's breathing was like a harnessed hurricane. He smiled as much in surprise at her speech as in amusement due to the protruding erection tenting out his trousers in Lydia's direction.

"Tonight, if possible," she added, gently touching his groin.

Ki's mind flashed, jumping between the disgusting warren he lived in and the Touchstone's back rooms for rent, but Lydia surprised him again.

"I don't want to stay here. Everybody knows me." She touched his finger and looked up at him. "My room has a separate entrance in the rear. Would that be all right?"

Ki figured it was a rhetorical question and had started to walk when she stopped him again.

"Ki, you understand I'm no virgin."

"Neither am I," he replied.

As the lamplight brightened over a table, her apartment proved to be a neatly dressed two-room suite of dark greens, satin, and fringe. Tassels hung from a gas lamp on the ceiling and from sconces. Hats decorated with long feathers and cocked brims hung from a stand. Inviting him in, Lydia carried a candle to the bedroom, and soon that room was suffused in soft golden light. She served Ki a drink from a well-kept selection atop a serving table and invited him to share the small couch with her.

It was impossible for Ki to keep his hands off Lydia for long once even casual contact had been made. He could smell her perfume and an attractive musk near her arms. Ki took note when she picked up his glass by mistake and drank it nearly empty. Putting the glass down, she realized what she had done and laughed brightly. She bent to retrieve it, offering to refill it for him, but Ki refused, and when she turned, their faces were close and their lips were parted. Lydia let her moist, open mouth fall upon Ki's lips, and they forgot entirely about drinking.

Ki's hands swept her dress from her shoulders and bared her great, pendulous breasts, which he gently massaged. He tickled her small pink nipples with the tip of his tongue until they hardened, then took each one in his mouth to suckle noisily. His hot tongue traveled into the chasm between her juglike mammaries, and he took each one in hand, softly stroking, tickling, and teasing. Lifting them from beneath, he pushed her nipples close enough together for him to suck and nibble both at once.

As if there were a nerve connecting her nipples to her crotch, Lydia's pelvis began to writhe, while Ki shifted on top of her. Her hands groped down his washboard stomach to feel the rock-hard pole-cock hidden within his denim. She pushed him back into his seat and was kneeling between his legs in a moment. As soon as she could unleash his raging hard-on, she swallowed it until her nose was in his hair and his glans had nowhere else to go. She threw her head up and down voraciously while holding his cock straight and stiff from its base. It glistened with her saliva dribbling down from her thick, soft lips as she made him groan with the teasing rasp of her tongue. Again she pumped madly, then shook her head from side to side during a slow withdrawal. She looked to see Ki in a seizure of pleasure while she rubbed the knob of his glans with her palm, sending sparks of tickling excitement through his body. She wiggled it sharply, the wetness feeling chill to Ki, until she dropped her head once more, slurping in every throbbing inch and moaning loudly.

"Do you like that?" she whispered. "Hmm? And you like my big nannies, Ki?" Stroking his erection gently with one hand, she smiled and said, "Hold that pose," and darted off to the bedroom. She returned instantly with a small corked

93

bottle. Stepping out of her dress, she knelt again before Ki.

She uncorked the bottle and poured a spot of clear, fragrant oil onto her palm. She worked the oil into both hands then onto Ki's engorged penis, moving her hands tauntingly, slowly, warming the oil by friction. She paused and added more oil to her palms, this time oiling the insides of her huge breasts down to the nipples. As Ki teased the pink knobs, Lydia squeezed her breasts around his shining cock and began to hump them up and down its length, watching its purple head thrust through her cleavage until a crystal bead of fluid danced on the tip.

For Lydia, this was almost too good to be true. She indulged her desire to please, growing more excited by the minute. She found herself really liking this man who spoke to her respectfully, understandingly. But she reminded herself that she also had a job to do.

She slowed to a stop. She sat back on her heels, never quite lifting her hand from his genitals.

"Ki, we don't really know each other. Do you think this is wrong?"

She let him suffer with that one a moment, then:

"It feels so right to me, I want to do this real bad. But I don't even know you. Am I bad?"

He thought a second and said, "You ain't no worse than I am. And since you think I'm so damn sweet, we must be doing something right."

She began stroking him lightly.

"Why didn't you come to Redemption a long while ago?" she said. "I can't believe we met, just like that. Tell me the truth, Ki, where did you come from?"

"I told you. I've lived in Colorado for years, down Animas way."

"Must be that hard work in the mines keeping you so strong and lean," she mused, while beginning to run her tongue up and down the underside of his cock. "And I hear you're one hell of a mountain lion when it comes to fighting."

Ki paused in his breathing. He sat up, staring her in the eye.

"Who ever told you such a thing?" he asked.

The split second Lydia's eyes traveled was long enough for him to know that what she was about to say was less than truth.

"This here mining town's a small one. In my line of work you hear gossip all the time."

In a soft, warm voice, Ki said, "Then you must hear all the gossip about your being Padgett's kept woman. How you must be his secret lover because, it's true, you're not like the other girls. And you probably know more about how the Gore Company works than anyone besides Padgett.

"And then there are things that most people probably never see when they look at you: a pretty woman with secrets to hide, who could make someone a fine companion someday. But she don't believe she deserved it, maybe because she feels damaged or not good enough. Maybe because she's too good and lets people walk all over her. I see pretty eyes that are really full of fear, that show hate and love for the same people. The extra-flashy clothes, the jewelry, the lovely cleavage, all get the attention you're afraid no one would give you any other way. A little too much rouge—covering up a bruise perhaps?"

He was hitting the mark like an archer bearing down. Lydia's attempt at a stern, defiant face was lined with the subtle musculature of sadness and hurt. She fought to appear insulted, not exposed. She shook her head in mock disbelief.

"You son of a bitch, do you really think . . . I can't believe you'd . . ." Her loss for words reflected the box she was in, nowhere else to go. Tears welled in her eyes, and though Ki knew tears could signal anger in women, this time he knew they didn't.

"I think you're a good person who gets used a lot, Lydia. Who doesn't get the respect you deserve, not for your thoughts, not for your work, and sure as hell, not for your body. You want to please everyone so much and be liked that sometimes you're not sure if you're dwindling away to nothing, all dried out and used up."

She broke down crying, and Ki pulled her up and hugged her tight, drawing out intense sobs that came deep and heavy, as if they had been dammed up for a long, long time. He soothed her and commiserated, confirming her fear that most other men in Redemption wouldn't throw a cow chip for anyone else's feelings, much less her own.

Getting herself together, Lydia stood up, obviously feeling twice as bad now for trying to take advantage of someone so nice. She blamed and cursed herself for her shortcomings until she realized how ridiculous she sounded, and sat beside Ki once again.

"You don't need to tell Padgett anything about me, Lydia. Someday you're going to have to stand up to him. You're the one who lets him use you."

Although she had little to say, she stayed close to his body, holding his arm with two hands as if for dear life.

"If you'd prefer to be alone," Ki said, "I'll go."

"No! Please. I'm sorry I cursed at you. C.C.'s the son of a bitch, not you. Please." She touched his chest with her fingertips. "I'd like you to stay." She managed a smile and added, "You really are nice."

They kissed, softly at first, then more passionately. Lydia rose and turned out the lamp. Passing slowly, she took Ki's hand and led him to the bedroom.

"I don't think I'd mind folks gossiping about you and me," she said.

She stood with him in the dim candlelight and unclothed him. His erection returned in a moment, and removing her remaining garments, Lydia lay back across her bed and spread her fleshy thighs. Her light brown pubic hair was thin and trimmed so short Ki could see her entire vulva, open and waiting. He crawled over her and gently lowered himself into her warmth, kissing her hotly.

"While you're screwing me," she whispered, "could we pretend we're making love?"

In affirmation, Ki's tongue slid down her neck to her breasts, and again he tasted her nipples. With one hand, he pressed the tip of his penis against her clitoris and massaged it side to side, causing her to pant and buck. Her feet went into the air as she tried to pull him in, but he teased her by not entering. Instead he dropped to his knees and took as much of her sex into his mouth as he could, flattening his tongue against her pearl, drenching it in saliva, drawing his tongue up lightly and driving her wild. She pulled his hair and stroked him. When he thrust his pointed tongue inside her fluid vagina, she pressed his head firmly against herself, rubbing her clitoris with his nose. She cried out and pulled him up by the shoulders repeating, "I want you, I want you now."

He slid his tongue up her belly, between her breasts and into her mouth as his bolt-hard erection parted her labia and probed deep into her heat. He drew up his knees, and she wrapped her legs around him. Curled like nested seashells, they humped powerfully until their juices ran down their legs and buttocks, until they could no longer kiss for want of air, until together they were wracked by the awesome power of simultaneous orgasms. Jetting copious amounts of hot semen into Lydia, Ki fell more deeply into her as her heels dug into his ass, spurring him to completion as if he were a stud horse.

Ki rolled off, and they held each other until the chill air drove them beneath the bed covers. Lydia's eyes smiled.

"That almost never happens for me," she admitted. "That was magic."

She seemed lost in thought for a long while afterward. Then she said, "You have to stay as far away from Padgett and his men as you can, Ki. Promise. I don't know exactly what he's up to, but with him and that Ryde Benton, things could get bad. Real bad. It would be best for you and that Starbuck woman to put Redemption behind you."

97

She thought more and worried her lip. "Watch out special for that Ryde Benton. He won't never stop. The miners, what they say is, 'The farther up the street you go, the tougher they get, and that Ryde Benton lives in the very last house.' "

In the days that followed, armed reprisals were traded between both mining companies. The Gore rabble swore vengeance upon the "Never Sleep killers." Grand River renegades retaliated for the ranch-house shootings—against Atwood's wishes—and to deter trespassers near the mines. *The Telegraph*, in its magnanimous striving "to better our scenic mountain village," made no effort to disguise its editorial bias against the Grand River operations, calling for investigations that never materialized, condemning violence as the paranoid reaction of corrupt and failing businessmen, and making thinly veiled threats against Atwood himself, in the form of vague but unmistakable references to the notorious use of vigilantes in taming towns like Denver and Lawrence. The position taken by *The Telegraph* and its gang of businessmen stunk of Company policy, which was Padgett's policy, and most folks knew it: Redemption was having its own civil war.

No one was killed in any raid. The only things that made contact with flying lead were replaceable or would grow back. But the level of anxiety the feuding instilled was intensely high—almost as high as the level of snobbery among those Redeemed who wanted Redemption to emulate Deadwood or Dodge. Almost as intense as their lust for all-out war should the attacks continue. That blood lust drove some folks far from Redemption, as those who'd seen John Coleson last said it had him. The warning that Benton and Kyle had administered to the tall blond—the boys at the Lodgepole generally agreed—was the lump of coal that topped off his car. But they weren't the very last ones to see him around; nor was Klue, the assayer, as many thought.

Klue was a nauseating stickler for details. The kind who kept every hair of his thick, square-cut goatee in place and loved paperwork more than testing even the richest ore. Working at his high desk in the Gore Assay Office, he never raised his head from his current assay report on Witless ore samples when Coleson walked past his window. The office faced the music hall and the #3 smelter, so Klue habitually blocked out the activity on the street.

Coleson casually walked by the low, whitewashed building with the long array of painted-over windows, carrying a couple of his spurious guides in his hand. The area around the telegraph pole out front, a magnet for Blossom Rock Guardsmen, stood vacant, this being around the time when most militiamen were on the switchbacks guarding samples or in the mines. Coleson saw no one at the side entrance, no one loitering around the small drums of chemicals and ceramic supplies piled there. And best of all, no Benton. He made a slow loop at the end of the street, seeing a few uniforms standing far back of the office, talking, spitting. He paused to view the scenery then doubled back.

He headed straight for the side entrance and picked up two 5 pound drums of soda ash. With a coin, he partially pried up the lid on one of them, then he came around to the front of the building. He put out his foot to open the door. Scratched into it was "Klue is a welch."

Figures, thought Coleson.

He moved into the office with only a nod to the assayer, who barely glanced up. Moving slowly, Coleson took an accurate scan of the room. Klue was pressing his pen hard into the paper to make a clear carbon copy of his report. To the right of Klue's desk, the office was divided from the workstation and supply shelves by a waist-high wooden balustrade with a hinged gate piece near the front. The wide-open gate was latched back against the rail on a spring hinge. Without hesitation, Coleson set the two drums down upon the rail top near the latch, being careful that the partially opened drum evenly straddled both rail and gate. Pretending the drums were cumbersome, or that he was especially inept, he squatted low enough to hook a finger

99

under the latch, flipping it open and clumsily shuffling his heels to disguise the sound.

"Don't leave that there," Klue whined after he signed his name and tore the report from the papers beneath it.

Coleson whistled. "This sure is some place you got here!" In an exaggerated bumpkin's tone he exclaimed, "I been to some assay offices since I been deliverin' this stuff, but, *hooey!* don't this beat all!" Klue slid the carbon into a waste bin at his feet and tried to interrupt, but Coleson baffled him. "You already know you was sent the wrong soda, I reckon. That's right, the boss said I should scoot right over to let you know, cuz you was sent the wrong soda." Klue rose from his seat, and Coleson said, "Here, allow me to show you." He lifted the closed drum and noticed that the gate had already begun to pull away from the rail under the spring's tension. The straddling five-pound drum was all that slowed it down.

"See?" he said, holding out the other drum. "This here ain't the grade o' soda yew need. That is to say, what's inside ain't right. Y'see, back where they pack the stuff, they ran outta the tins that your soda wuz suppose to git into, then they wuz set aside, see, after they filled 'em, and when the right ones—your'n—when the right ones come in, wouldn't you know them clunks put in the wrong soda. Leastways, that's as good as the boss and me cin figger. Fact, we ain't rightly sure which kind o' soda's in this here tin, compared to what kind o' soda you got on yer shelfs right now. Which is why the boss send me scootin' over. To make it all clarified to you, personal."

"What in hell are you palavering about?" Klue scoffed. "Can't you see what it says right there on the—"

"Never had no schoolin' in letters, sir, I'm sorely frightened to say, but my mama . . ."

"If you can't read, what are you doing with those pamphlets?"

"Oh, these, somebody jest slip me a couple, case I knew someone what would care to have one."

"Give me the tin!" Klue snatched the container from his hand and set it down to pry it open with a knife.

"My mama was a good-hearted lady who learned me Bible stories by recitin' 'em and likewise her mama before—"

"This looks exactly like the soda ash we always use." said Klue. "Are you sure you're in the right state?"

"The boss sez to me, 'You tell them at Gore they'd best double compare this here tin agin what they got on their shelfs,' so that's what I'm here to tell you. You'd best double comp—"

"Give me that!"

Tin in hand, Klue huffed back to his inventory shelves. Simultaneously, in one long step, Coleson reached the waste bin, swiped two pieces of carbon paper, and pocketed them before Klue even reached them.

"I know how confused things must get here," Coleson called out, "with all this here science stuff. Yew cin figger fer yerself how confused we are, the boss and me."

"Easily," came Klue's voice as he selected a tin from a shelf. By the time he had it opened, Coleson had pilfered a blank assay report that had been beneath the one Klue worked on last and slipped it between the pages of a booklet. Another booklet he held high.

"I'm gonna leave this here book fer you, sir!" he called. He noticed that the gate had pulled so far from the rail as to leave the tin resting on its very edges. "I reckon you'd more'n likely make some sense of it. I hear tell there's somethin' to learn there."

"Don't do me any favors," Klue said from the back of the room. Finally he added, "Now, I don't know where in God's creation you got the idea that this is the wrong soda ash!" and started back toward Coleson carrying two tins. As he neared the rail, the hinge spring flexed the final bit necessary to pull the gate out from under the weight of the drum, sending it crashing to the floor to burst into a cloud of white powder. With a cry of surprise, Coleson sprung forward and lifted it—upside down—spilling the ash over

101

a wide area that included Klue's trousers and shoes.

"Damn you! Stupid cracker! Imbecile!" Klue was beside himself with anger, and the bumbling intruder wouldn't stop apologizing. "Get out! Leave before you say another word!"

"Awful sorry, sir," Coleson said, patting himself and heading for the door. "I'll be sure to tell the boss to see you 'bout this personal," and out he flew.

Klue was not the last one to see Coleson before he skipped town because, after his little performance at the Assay Office, Coleson was next seen at the livery stable just before nightfall. He paid in full for the more than two weeks' he stabled his Appaloosa there. The proprietor, a grizzled old coot named Grimes, remembered thinking it strange to see a citified pantywaist like Coleson riding a fine Appaloosa in these rugged hills. But then, Grimes seldom bathed, and that seemed perfectly normal to him.

By dark of night, Coleson put some tracks between himself and Redemption, and no one thought it strange. If a stray piece of lead thrown during a nuisance raid didn't kill him, Benton probably would. Just for the hell of it.

★

Chapter 9

"Carriage coming up the drive, Judge!"

Atwood looked up from his papers at the call from Rosilda's kid. The boy held the front door ajar and anxiously waited for him to come. The kid's voice had been sounding nervous and excited only since the trouble began. As Atwood stood in the doorway, he put a reassuring hand on the boy's shoulder. Darnell, one of Atwood's better young men, was already on his feet with his carbine in the crook of his arm. He showed no weariness from the long hours he had spent sitting in the chair out front, on watch. Darnell's teenaged brother, Will, peeked from around the corner of the building.

The hansom, drawn by a fine-looking paired team, was well kept, and the driver wore a suit. There were only a few men in the area who rode in such comfort, Atwood knew, and all of them worked for Gore. Sure enough, as the carriage rounded the path's winding curves, Atwood recognized the pale, mustachioed face of Padgett. Beside him sat two others.

Rosilda's kid steadied the team when they had stopped. Padgett waited for his driver to open his door and stepped down, looking uncomfortable. Kyle the shift boss and a guy Atwood recognized as a reporter for *The Telegraph* followed. Atwood had to force himself to approach them civilly.

"And what brings you folks such a long way this morning?" he asked.

"Judge Atwood," said Padgett, extending a gloved hand. The judge shook it perfunctorily, displeased. "I have come to have a word with you, about resolving our differences. Would you welcome us into your home?"

Officious ass, Atwood thought, but always the gentleman, he said, "Of course," and showed them into his wide front room. "See to the horses," he said to Rosilda's kid.

Accepting the tea Rosilda served, Padgett was obviously trying to appear congenial. Atwood had known the man long enough to recognize his discomfort, his badly disguised condescension. Padgett seemed to dither about removing his gloves before taking up his teacup, but finally he did. Then out came the requisite monogrammed silk handkerchief, his trademark quirk.

After recapping the series of reprisals and nuisance raids, Padgett reaffirmed his dislike for violence and his commitment to high business ideals. He proposed an end to the violence and a new consolidation of all mining interests in the region.

"You mean you'd like to absorb the Grand River operations into your own," Atwood stated.

"Not exactly," Padgett replied. "It would be a cooperative merger. It would take advantage of the Gore Company's existing facilities which, being more extensive and superior to your Grand River facilities, would be a sizeable asset to you. And it would put fewer people out of work. You would maintain some control and benefit from the proceeds."

"Some control," Atwood repeated. "Just how much is 'some'?"

"The precise details can be worked out another time. I

am here to invite you to a formal peace offering. On neutral ground, so to speak."

This came as a surprise to Atwood, but looked like a predictably diplomatic opening to a very hostile takeover. In Atwood's eyes, Gore Mining and Milling was on its way to paying out, a business doomed to fail as the lodes were depleted, the timber stripped away, the work force moved elsewhere. The reasons for not accepting the invitation were grounded in Atwood's deep suspicion of Padgett's business motives, and in Atwood's confidence in his own ability to protect Grand River Mining. However, the reasons for accepting a common-ground offering, he had to admit, were compelling, he being a man of peace and this possibly being an opportunity to calm the tensions in the gulch before somebody else got killed.

"And what about the Never Sleep disaster?" Atwood asked. "Are you willing to admit that we had nothing to do with that?"

Kyle sighed loudly and sneered, but Padgett silenced him with a glance. The reporter simply stood by listening, never taking a note or asking a question.

"While it was clearly arson and there was some very incriminating evidence that the culprit works for you, I am willing to let the official investigation determine who was responsible without interference or bias. But getting to the bottom of the Never Sleep killings will take time. Meanwhile I don't want this town to blow up in my face. For everyone's sake."

"Agreed. What did you have in mind?" Atwood ventured.

"Breaking bread together, your people, my people, our families. We'll share a meal which my company will pay for. We'll present our ideas and have an open discussion to weigh both sides and work out a solution."

"Like a picnic," Kyle added.

"Yes," said Padgett, "like one of those church luncheons you see back east. We could put people's minds at ease and get down to real business, too. I believe we could find a solution."

Atwood was pensive, careful.

"Who would attend?" he asked.

"Anyone you'd like," Padgett shrugged. "Fifty, a hundred people, whatever; but certainly your decision-making executives. Bring your family. We will do the same. *The Telegraph* will be there to abstract the proposals for the public in its next edition. We could do it, say, three days from now?"

It sounded to Atwood like politics. Public posturing to make Padgett look like the good guy, the conciliator. Well, so what? he figured. He wasn't about to give up any part of his business, and maybe his somewhat tarnished public image would be polished in joining. If it turned into an open debate, so be it: Atwood could debate with the best of them and not be humiliated.

Three locations were offered, all of them more or less equally distant from Atwood's ranch and Redemption, about a morning's ride. All three were wide open, treeless pastures with long, visible approaches. It would be Atwood's choice.

Standing before Padgett, looking typically dignified, Judge Atwood offered his hand to accept the invitation, his mind squirming at the sight of his diminutive guest wringing his handkerchief. They shook on it and quickly deliberated over some minor details, Padgett adding, as if it were an afterthought, "I intend to instruct my men to leave even the most inoffensive weapon at home." The Gore Company president then made a hasty exit, eliciting long sighs and snide remarks from both sides.

Atwood himself delivered his choice of location to the Gore offices next day. He asked to see Padgett in person, but was turned away as Padgett was "conducting business at home and would be unavailable all day." He left his calling card. On the street, all eyes were upon him, and he sensed they were filled as much with hope as with fear. It was

106

always the regular folks who reacted to things they didn't understand with deeds they could only poorly explain, in situations they didn't create, only to suffer the consequences almost entirely alone. Considering folks' fears and misinformed peeves, Atwood traveled the entire way home with his fully loaded Winchester on his lap and more ammunition in his pocket.

Friday, the day of the "powwow," as many Redeemed called it, dawned leaden. Arvilla and Jessie were up and about before Judge Atwood had planned to wake them, and by the time they were outdoors, Darnell and Will were already waiting in the buckboard. The older brother's breath rose in slow-moving clouds. Atwood and the two young ladies joined them. In the yard, two other wagons waited, loaded with baskets and barrels and nearly a score of men and women trying to stay warm. Taking their lead from Atwood's wagon, they set off, twenty-three people in all, for the long ride to the valley of Smoking Earth River.

By mid-morning, the wagons had been pushed and pulled and practically lifted along the rugged trails at least three times. In their shirtsleeves, men walked rather than climbed in and out of the wagons each time they stopped. Beneath shimmering stands of aspen, the undergrowth was scorched and the ground crusty, having been long without rain. The sound of distant thunder drew folks' eyes skyward, but no rain came.

The pasture, an outlying parcel belonging to an old acquaintance of Atwood's, was a good half mile wide, river to tree line, with no rise to speak of. Smack in the middle stood three wagons curved around blankets spread on the ground. People milled about, setting crates and barrels down, tending a grill pit at one end. Atwood led his train around the unoccupied side of the blankets and stepped down.

The big man, Ryde Benton, stood to the center of the blankets, and waved with a smile. Kyle, the Decatur kid, and Big Dave the Dog-eater stood nearby and, off to one side, was Ki, surprised to have been brought along at Benton's request.

Standing tall a few feet from Benton, Atwood asked, "Where's Mr. Padgett?"

"Mr. Padgett regrets not bein' here," Benton said. "His health ain't been right, and he don't cotton to travel much no more. But he gave me authority to do business with you." He extended his beefy hand, and Atwood shook it. "But let's eat first. C'mon, sit down."

He called everyone down from the wagons and invited them to where log-and-plank benches had been arranged. They gathered loosely around Atwood and sat. Slabs of beef and buffalo were already sizzling on the grills and pots of coffee gave off their rich aroma. Only three of Benton's fifteen people were women, but to Jessie, the few women on Benton's side of the blankets were hardly ladies. They looked calloused and tough as rawhide. Including women in the proceedings was meant as a sign of good will; these folks only filled Jessie with dread and a desire to get them bathed. When most were settled, Benton approached Atwood with a ceremonial Ute pipe, beautifully carved in catlinite, its long stem decorated with shiny nail heads. Benton and his cohorts smiled when he posed to make a speech.

"I'd like to commence with this here pipe . . . ," he turned playfully to his men, " . . . which I got from a Yampa chief direct. Nice fellow—no longer with us, sad to say." Chuckles rustled behind him. "Them Utes smoke pipes before talkin' business—maybe throw back a drink or two, I venture—and I think we should, too. To show no hard feelin's."

Amid silence, he struck a match and puffed heavily on the pipe. Finally he drew a great breath and let the smoke drift lazily from his mouth and nostrils. With a gasp, he pulled the smoke in deeper and swayed his head from side to side, sending billowing white spirals into the breeze. With one hand, he even waved some of the smoke over

108

his head, "Like the red men do," he said with a wide smile. Finally he offered Atwood the pipe. The judge accepted, never taking his eyes from his host.

"Mr. Byrd," Benton called out to *The Telegraph* reporter, "how about serving our guests some coffee?" And soon tin cups of the bitter brew were being passed around. With a wave of his hand, Benton called for two spitted buffalo steaks, and handing one to Atwood, he said, "Here's to settling our differences," and took a ravenous bite.

The large, succulent steaks were distributed while Atwood seemed to play with his. Standing among barrels near the wagons, Benton's men took none of the meat until all of Atwood's people had theirs.

"Don't wait for us," Benton said. "No one else would."

Standing among Benton's men, Ki sensed gradual movements among them. Johnny Talbot, the tall kid with greasy hair and bad complexion, drifted away from the grills and closer to the buckboard. Kyle was busy piling loaves of sourdough from a small barrel onto a blanket he knelt beside. The Gore men seemed nervous to Ki, while Atwood's indulged themselves in the feast. Only Atwood and Jessie were vigilant.

The owner of a ranch on the other side of the river, a gambling man named Jeb Sully, was yammering about how good the prospecting should be west of Redemption— generally toward Atwood's holdings. While he spoke, no one paid much attention to the first guttural noise coming from a miner beside Atwood. But after one of the women, then another man bent over in choking gags, Atwood sprang up. Seeing his people doubling over, he shouted, "Don't eat anything!" and threw his spit to the ground.

No sooner had Atwood focused upon his host than Benton leveled a well-concealed knuckle-duster at him, an ugly, barrel less .22 caliber Reid revolver that didn't need to be accurate to be lethal at so close a range. As if expecting it, Atwood rolled to one side just as one of his poisoned employees threw himself before Benton's gun, taking the lead through the face, below his right eye. Someone threw Benton a fist, drawing the big man's fire away from the judge.

Gunfire exploded simultaneously from every man behind Benton. The Grand River folks began to scatter, but it was like shooting fish in a barrel for the attackers. Several of Atwood's people, cringing in the gut-wrenching throes of poisoning, were shot dead where they fell. The revolver Kyle pulled from the sourdough keg was one Ki had never seen before. It looked like a Peacemaker but smaller, with a short barrel and bird's head grip. When Kyle commenced throwing hot lead into the backs of two fleeing women, Ki realized it was one of those fancy self-cockers. Without pause, Kyle squeezed off another three rounds, and because he was a poor shot, only one more man fell. Amid teams of skittish, bucking horses, Sully steadied the twenty-inch barrel of his Winchester carbine on the sideboard of a wagon. With more than a dozen chances to kill at his fingertips, he bore down on his defenseless prey, as cool as a winter wind off the azure hogbacks in the distance.

Just then Ki caught sight of the Talbot kid drawing a bead on Atwood, who was struggling to his feet after Benton's first kill. There was no mistaking the old rifle Talbot wielded or the danger it posed. The side hammer on the Colt revolving rifle had barely twitched before Ki knocked it skyward and came down with a thundering elbow to Talbot's stomach. He yanked Talbot to his feet and slammed him furiously against the buckboard. Talbot surprised the tall warrior with a fist like a silver ingot to the abdomen, which doubled Ki over and nearly winded him for good. Short of that, it merely enraged him. He thrust upward and bashed the kid's jaw with the back of his head. There was a shivering crack of tooth upon tooth. With a swoop, one of Atwood's men retrieved the weapon. Voicing a chilling spirit yell, Ki pummeled Talbot to the ground with a series of snapping full-fisted blows to the body and across the temple, then ducked aside to assess the calamity. Before quitting the unconscious mucker, Ki noticed the canvas ammo pouch slung beneath Talbot's vest, yanked it off, and stashed it inside his shirt.

Firing the revolving rifle from the hip, Atwood's man instantly dropped the Decatur kid dead with a bullet in the head. But the cylinder's fierce lateral blast ignited a neighboring chamber in the same breath, the stray discharge maiming the man's forward hand and bringing the rifle to the ground once again.

Amid the confusion, Ki got to the Colt first. If he had counted right, there'd be three shots left—maybe just enough to keep the zigzagging Atwood alive until he cleared the stand of piñon pine at the edge of the meadow. What he hadn't noticed was Sully taking aim at him from a kneeling position just a few yards off. But Arvilla, having skirted the killing ground in an effort to reach the river, did notice. She had seen Ki save Atwood's life as well, and suddenly understood who this long-haired man was. Drawing an antler-handled blade from the top of her boot, she hurled herself at Sully with a scream that chilled his blood and shook his aim. The blade came down in a two-handed power thrust into the exposed side of his neck, carving a fatal gash clear through the center. Without breaking her stride, Arvilla had Sully's rifle in one hand, her knife in the other, and was racing alongside Ki like a wild filly. Sully's life flowed into the rich Colorado soil he coveted so much, while his body twitched and his cries drowned in the thick gurgle of blood in his windpipe.

After Benton's foiled attempt on Atwood's life, he succeeded in emptying his gun into the backs of two other Grand River miners as they tried to ford the river. Inky red clouds billowed around their bodies before vanishing in the sun-sparkled waters. But his next target surprised him. Darnell was the lone Grand River man packing iron for the feast. And before two Gore men could fan off four shots between them, Darnell's spur-trigger Smith & Wesson revolver brought them down.

111

Checking his left flank, Benton now found himself staring into Darnell's deadly octagonal barrel. But it wasn't his time to die. Pulling off balance the first man within arm's reach—a mineral-stained miner named Ware—Benton put himself on the far side of danger by putting Ware between himself and the bullet. At the moment of Ware's death, a stray shot tore a deep, slanting gash across the inside of Darnell's thigh. His pain-wracked escape, aided by his dedicated younger brother and bought with a desperate hail of lead that emptied his pistol, seemed even to him nothing less than a miracle.

Ki made good his and Arvilla's escape with a minimum of firing, skirting wide along the river, then toward the treeline. He held the unwieldy old Colt with both hands behind the receiver, keeping the buttstock low to his chest. Benton's gang must not have wanted Ki dead, for it would have been a cinch. At least one gunman, Ki noticed, was firing a well-kept Yellow Boy. Aiming calmly, the killer simply marched forward, firing at the retreating targets without so much as a squint. Jessie, Atwood, and their people ran like hell, becoming more alarmed as one after another of their friends fell jaw-first beside them. Once into the woods, no one slowed down until someone noticed they weren't being followed. Deeper in they ran. Names were called to find out who was missing.

The shooting died down in less than five minutes. The echoes seemed to last longer. With lungs burning, the survivors gathered from many directions, shocked, disbelieving. Young Will appeared, practically dragging his wounded brother. Ki and Arvilla startled them with their arrival from their flank. Only six remained.

Breathless and frantic, Jessie tried to form words but only bellowed. She slapped the trees and held her head, but knew they had to keep moving. When she saw Ki, she called his name and grasped Arvilla's hand. She urged them on.

Leaving his brother on the ground, Will threw himself against Ki in a violent rage, thinking Ki was one of

Benton's killers. Jessie grappled with them, but alone she could barely prevent the capable young fighter from doing damage to the reluctant warrior. Atwood stood forward, and it took the man several minutes to calm the deranged boy. With a weathered frown, Atwood insisted, "He saved my life, he's not one of them!" Will stared back, his chest still heaving. Tears welled up in his eyes, and he fell back to his brother.

Jessie was already tearing Darnell's calico shirt into strips to dress his wound. Gently wiping away some of the blood, she wrapped the leg, and gathering two strips in either hand, she drew them down into a square knot. Darnell winced without a sound. Beads of sweat glistened on his brow.

With help from Will, Darnell rose to his feet and tested his leg. When he looked up at Ki, the warrior knew he was looking into the eyes of a dead man. They set off toward the ranch with Darnell leaning on his brother's shoulder. It looked to Ki like a three-legged race, and it made him glance over his shoulder more often than he cared to.

It became brutally apparent that Darnell's condition was worsening by the minute. Though he bore his pain in proud silence, the bleeding had not slowed. It was a red river. His lower leg began to swell. The entire group's progress was retarded, and there was no telling whether Benton's posse would be pursuing. Ki knew something had to be done.

Arvilla walked close by Ki. She said nothing. When their eyes met, Ki saw the anger in her mask of grief. He wondered how much of her stoicism was facade, how much was pure, distilled rage iced over by years of nearly lone survival. He was almost relieved to see, when she snatched a secret glance, a single tear crystallize on her lash. Arvilla blinked it back and assumed a mask of bravery.

From the edge of a dense wood, the group looked out over a small lake. Beside them, a clear-running stream tumbled through the steep wood and across the meadow below. Beyond, a towering, majestic flattop amphitheater reigned silently over the expanse of mountain and sky, dwarfing immense lodgepole pines clinging to its colossal slopes. Here they decided to rest.

Having splashed stream water on his face and neck, Ki sat apart from the others. Darnell's pain was becoming difficult to hide. Ki stooped and drank, then eased himself close to Jessie, whose face was lined with worry.

"That leg needs fixin'," he suggested. "Looks real bad."

Jessie breathed deeply and cast up her eyes. She nodded in agreement. "I know," she whispered, "but not here." It took her a few moments to gain some composure, and putting one hand upon Ki's knee, she sighed, "Let's go."

As Jessie picked up her pace ahead of him, Ki stared intently at her glossy honey-colored hair loosely gathered behind her. Jessie was easily the most remarkable woman Ki had ever known, and he would have done anything for her. His dedication was limitless; he felt honored to be charged with her protection. Seldom had he ever imagined a woman so ready to court death for an honorable cause— and never a woman so utterly enticing as she, although becoming anything more than her protector was a blessing that was forever denied him. Deep down, he knew he would die for her.

They had walked barely another mile when they came within sight of a fast-moving creek across a wide field. Atwood suggested it was best not to ford the creek in daylight, so they paused by an outcropping of rock that would serve as a lookout. Jessie spoke quietly with the watery-eyed judge. She then approached Ki.

"Let's do that leg now."

When the bandage came away from the wound, it was obviously dirty and certain to become infected. A fresh rivulet of blood ran out of the deep gash and across swollen skin of a sickening blue-black color. Kneeling beside Darnell, Ki guessed the wound was too large to be cauterized with a hot blade. He hesitated a moment and looked up at Atwood. Then he pulled Talbot's ammo pouch from his shirt.

Removing a cartridge, he bit and twisted out the lead and widened the wound with his free hand. Darnell jolted at his touch. With a glance, Ki got the others to restrain Darnell's legs and torso. Will removed his elkskin belt and placed the edge between his brother's teeth.

Again Ki spread the wound, then he poured the cartridge's gunpowder into it. By Darnell's grunts and writhing, they knew it stung something awful. Ki repeated the process with another cartridge. Patting down his own shirt, he produced a match. Darnell bit down hard on the leather, tightened his face, and took a deep breath.

"Stand back some," Ki said, before striking the match across his thigh.

The wound ignited in a sibilant flash. Darnell bucked upward, nearly throwing off all three who held him down. Ki heard the flash sizzle amid Darnell's savage growls and could smell gunpowder and burning flesh intermingled.

It was done. Darnell fainted into a deep sleep that was sure to last awhile. The fugitive party prepared to bed down as best they could. Sitting with his back to a tree, Ki broke down the temperamental old Colt and tried to clean it. As he loaded the sixth chamber, he swore under his breath. The old iron seemed nearly useless to him, with its outdated ammunition and poorly sealed chambers. He looked through its upraised barrel and suddenly felt eyes upon him. He turned to see Arvilla's sad gaze in the fading light. She turned away and nestled down to rest, leaving Ki with an empty sense of want that seemed trivial before the danger lying ahead.

★

Chapter 10

"You drunken old fool, you've got to do something!" Jessie screamed only inches away from Sheriff Nettles's face. Veins showed in her temples, and Nettles could smell the sweat that had dried on her after nearly two days without sleep. "They murdered seventeen innocent people, shot them down in cold blood, and what are you doing here but sucking down that god-awful swill and believing trouble's just gonna ride away!" She pulled at his shirt as he sat glued to his chair, stuttering uselessly, trying to calm his irate visitor, whose voice weakened with futility. "Damn it, Sheriff, don't you see? It was a damned slaughter!"

Jessie released his shirt as if she had been touching filth and dropped into a wooden chair beside the sheriff's desk. Her eyes were bloodshot. She wiped the sweat from her face and swept back her disheveled hair. The late-summer humidity was almost as bad as in West Texas.

"What are you going to do?" she asked.

Nettles leaned forward, stammering on about an investigation, questioning whose jurisdiction it was out there by the Smoking Earth, advising reason and a calm approach.

116

His impotence became explicit when he dithered and complained about hiring deputies—who was there to hire in Redemption but employees of Benton and the Gore company?—because he would surely require help in handling such a case. He shuffled papers across his desk as if he were lost in them and repeated the need to stay calm, to not overreact. As weak and drained of energy as Jessie was, she felt she could easily tear out Nettles's cowardly heart with her bare hands and make him eat it.

It was Saturday, less than thirty hours since the slaughter. Redemption had looked like a ghost town when Jessie rode in on a deep-muscled bay gelding. Wearing her .38 in her gunbelt, she defied every voice of reason at the Atwood ranch and brazenly rode into town, certain that no one would dare attempt to harm her. There was at least a lawful facade in Padgett's little empire city. She barely saw a soul anywhere. Even the smelters, which normally screamed and spewed filth into the air day and night, seemed abnormally quiescent. There were no comings or goings along the switchback trails to the headframes and stamp mills except a few timid men scurrying about the buildings perched high atop the ridges. This entire horrid town is a slaughterhouse, Jessie thought, whether they murder you outright or you die in the bowels of the earth. And in his own, unresisting way, Nettles was a vile accomplice.

She told him so.

"Try to understand, Miss Jessie," Nettles began, rising to his feet, "this here town has a law all its own. And what am I? You sez it yerself: a drunk old fool. What can I do? What *you* gonna do? You can't fight 'em! Them folks that died yesterday ain't the first. Ain't the last, I'm sorry to say."

Jessie leapt up and cursed, threatening that she was not only capable of getting something done, but intent on it. Quickly Nettles lowered his voice to a pleading tone but didn't give an inch.

"Don't you hear, missy? Things gonna stay the way things is in this town, no countin' what nobody does, leastways

117

some purtty young outlander like you. Not even that pack o' vigilantes last year—that, that 'Committee o' Safety'—could clean it up! Now, let me commence to investigatin' this here mess and do things without no more dyin'!"

Jessie fumed quietly for a moment. When she spoke, the calm of her voice was more threatening than her shouts.

"You listen to me. Before the next full moon, I swear, I'll see every one of those ornery coyotes hogtied, hung, and hell-bound, and there ain't no one in this god-forsaken butthole of a town that'll stop me. With one telegraph, I'll have every sheriff's deputy in the county, every available stripe in Fort Steele, and every bounty-hunting gunslick north of the Canadian crawlin' up your backside—and the governor, too, if I gotta. I know the right people, and it's gonna happen, so help me."

No sooner had she tramped heavily out the door than another footstep sounded behind Nettles.

The weak-eyed sheriff turned and said, "She's gonna telegraph for all kinds o' hellfire and damnation, and I don't—"

"Ain't no telegraphs comin' out of Redemption," Benton said from the rear doorway. "Count on it, Kentucky." He lifted a flask of whiskey from his back pocket and uncorked it. Placing it down on the bottom shelf of the gun rack, he said, "And you ain't gonna waste your valuable time messin' with some dumb old 'vestigation. Now are ya, Virge?"

Nettles was crestfallen. He leaned back on his crowded desk, struggling to keep his eyes off the enticing flask. His silence Benton took to be an affirmation, and without another word, the death-dealing mine superintendent slipped out the back door, knowing that Nettles was likely to dive upon the whiskey like a desert dog at a water hole.

Skulking behind the buildings, Benton kept apace of Jessie as she led her bay by the bridle along Eagle Road. She tethered him and entered the telegraph office at the newspaper. Benton hurried across the street and down to he Lodgepole, guessing how long she'd be occupied. He failed to notice a tall blond in a wide-brimmed hat returning to town on an Appaloosa.

Coleson was wary about riding straight through the center of town, and just past the music hall, he turned off the main road to come up a side street. He left his mount tied to a sapling behind Nettles's office and walked around through the front carrying a small shoulder pouch. Startled, Nettles stole one last swig from the flask and dropped it, uncorked, into a file drawer. Coleson pretended not to see it.

"Howdie, Marshal."

Nettles couldn't talk for the fire in his throat. He grimaced while trying to swallow and beckoned Coleson in with his hand. Finally he coughed and said, "You got more rocks to show me, or somethin'?"

Coleson removed his hat and wrinkled his nose upon getting a whiff of the place. Flies buzzed in the late-day sunlight slanting through the barred window.

"No, Marshal, I'd like to parley with y'all about something that happened up there on the toll road outta Eagle."

"Must be a bad time o' year. Awright. Jest what kind o' trouble you got, son?"

Coleson let the marshal mosey behind his desk, figuring it made him feel important, and spoke casually about his trip to Eagle. He reminded Nettles about the guidebooks he sold, and produced a handful from his pouch. While telling a long-winded story about being charged too high a toll for carrying merchandise for sale, Coleson sauntered about, fiddling with a piece of paper, rolling it into a thin tube.

"Have a seat, why dontcha?" said Nettles as he slumped into his chair.

"Thanks," Coleson replied, but remained standing. "Now, I don't think it proper for private citizens like myself to be charged high tolls for a negligible commodity like this," he said, dropping a copy in front of the nervous old man, "and I think I got a mind to bring charges upon those folks who are evidently bilking passersby like me on that road."

119

"Have yerself a chair, mister," Nettles said, "and I'll hear your story."

"Thanks, Marshal. Say, ain't there no papers I gotta sign for charging somebody with something?"

Nettles dismissed the need for such formality and suggested the tall geologist give him some specifics. Instead, Coleson meandered toward the gun rack and inspected the firearms—two Colt Peacemakers, one with a chipped walnut grip, a Remington-Rider double-action, and a Remington No. 3. They lined the bottom of the rack, with a chain through the trigger guards that was locked at one side. Above them and similarly chained were four rifles. None of the weapons looked as if they had been used—or even cleaned—in a while. Coleson lifted the cork he found lying there.

"This something you need, Marshal?"

Nettles fumbled to his feet, "Uh . . . naw, that's jest from an old coal cil tin."

Smelling the cork, Coleson said, "Must taste awful nasty, that coal oil."

Nettles took the cork and headed back to his desk, mumbling. While his back was turned, Coleson slipped the rolled-up paper into the dusty octagonal barrel of the Remington-Rider. Nettles never suspected a thing.

Leaning over his desk, the marshal said more emphatically, "Now look, son, you gonna take a chair, or am I gonna have to lasso you to figger whar the shoe pinches?"

Coleson stood deep in thought.

"You know something, Marshal? After concentratin' on it, I'm of a mind to let this little incident blow over after all. Ain't proper for me to take up your valuable time over a little fuss like this. I'm assured it was just a misunderstanding. I apologize for abusin' your attention thusways."

And he gave Nettles's hand a few quick shakes and left.

"Well, I'll be damned," Nettles muttered.

When Jessie left the telegraph office, she found her horse missing. It wasn't hard to see by the prints in the soil that someone had led the bay downhill, so, checking her revolver, she hurried in that direction. With her hand on the pistol grip, she proceeded down the middle of the quiet road, gazing intently down the alleys between buildings. As she neared the livery stable, a door that had been ajar was pulled closed from inside. Jessie fought against her urge to freeze. She removed her Colt from its holster. Coming upon the alley alongside the stables, she saw movement at the rear of the building and halted. There was the bay lazily searching for something to graze, its reins hanging loose in the dust. With a glance all around her, Jessie cautiously walked in.

As she crept to the rear of the building, she could see the corral. The horses calmly kept their eyes upon her. Whispering to her bay, she noticed two of the corralled animals suddenly turn their eyes to her left. Simultaneously cocking her Colt and stepping forward, Jessie spun around, stopping Kyle the shift boss in mid-lunge, her revolver leveled at his forehead.

"That's my bay, and I'm taking him outta here," she said.

A door she hadn't noticed flew open and knocked her off her feet as she triggered the Colt. The report of the gun spooked the horses, but another man, appearing from behind, held her horse. Before she knew it, she was being whisked to her feet by the powerful Ryde Benton and dragged helplessly into the stable building. Kyle thrust her gun into the back of his pants and joined two other surly muckers inside, closing the door behind himself. Bringing her into an open shoeing area, Benton knocked her down again with an open hand that felt like a club.

"I seen some dumb bitches in my time," Benton growled in his deep, hollow voice, "but I ain't never knowed none so stupid as you, to come back after what happened yesterday." He stooped and grabbed a handful of her long, lustrous hair and pulled her to her feet. Jessie held tight to his wrist with both hands. Her outcry elicited curses from Benton and urges from his goons for him to hit her again. His face came close enough to hers to bathe her in his putrid breath while she stared into his inhuman, colorless eyes.

Jessie struggled to break his hold and kicked him in the shins. Benton's accomplices seized her arms and head, and Kyle hurt her by pulling one elbow too far back.

"Feisty little mare, ain't she!" Kyle exclaimed.

"Break her, Ryde, break her!" cried another.

Benton squeezed her mouth in one powerful hand.

"You don't come from 'round here, and you don't know shit about nothin'. I'll tell you right now, what happened yesterday ain't but the beginning. Three of my boys was put down, and I ain't gonna forget that. This here town belongs to us, you hear? And there ain't nothing you gonna do about it."

Jessie shook his hand loose and said, "What are you gonna do, kill me, too? Huh? A big man like you needing three clods to put down one woman? You cowardly piece of shit!"

Benton clamped down on her jaw once more and resisted hitting her. The others moaned and jeered, and she could feel their vile hands over her body. Kyle squeezed her breast painfully while someone's hand thrust between her thighs. She wriggled and fought them off to no avail.

Benton roared, "I'll break you all right!" and tore open her shirt, sending buttons flying. "Get her down!" he raged and threw her to the ground. "Get her arms!"

The two muckers dropped upon her, invading her cotton undergarment with their calloused hands while Kyle danced about, calling, "Screw her, Ryde! Screw her good!"

"This ain't screwing," Jessie squealed. "You're hurting me!"

Benton fell to his knees and slapped her hard. She aimed to kick him in the groin and thought she had hit her mark, but it just made him madder. She began screaming at a bloodcurdling pitch and calling for help. Benton slapped her again and choked her.

"You shut the hell up, hear me? Shut it!" He began undoing her gunbelt.

A gunshot exploded from the doorway, loud as thunder, and rang in their ears as dust fell from the roof. It was Coleson. The men jolted, and Kyle drew the Colt from behind him. Before he could cock it, the tall blond in the door dropped to one knee, a pistol in each hand, and triggered his right-hand weapon. This time, only the click of a misfire sounded. He veered to the ground just as Kyle fired. With a *spang*, the bullet ricocheted off an anvil, and Kyle groped to pull back the Colt's hammer. Coleson's left-hand revolver blazed as he rolled, shattering Kyle's gun hand and dropping the Colt to within Jessie's reach. Instinctively she kicked Benton in the chest and jumped for it. When Benton tried to beat her to it, Coleson yelled, "Don't!" and successfully fired from his right, the lead throwing up straw only inches in front of Benton's knee and sending the big man back on his haunches. Seizing the Colt, Jessie rolled away from the stunned miners and raised it.

Coleson stood, keeping his guns trained on his targets. Jessie noticed that the pistol in his right hand had a lanyard swivel on its butt. It was a trouble-prone double-action Colt Army. In his left he wielded a finely engraved pistol she didn't recognize right off—a Merwin Hulbert Army, a curvaceous weapon with top strap and fluted cylinder.

"You all right, Jessie?" Coleson asked.

She nodded. For a geologist, this guy can shoot! she thought.

"You fellas have had your fun," Coleson said in a level voice. "Now we're gonna back outta this town, and ain't none of you gonna follow. I'll put the first man who does six feet under."

There was no doubt in their minds that Coleson could back his play, so they just stood there and watched him and Jessie leave.

"Git on home with your mama's boy, slut," growled Benton. "I'll split you yet."

Coleson raised his Colt directly at Benton's nose, but the big man didn't flinch. His water-clear eyes stared with a coldness like the winds of hell. Jessie opened the door cautiously with her gun cocked and ready. Outside, Coleson closed the door and leaned a short rail against the handle. Finding Jessie's bay in the corral, they hightailed it out of Redemption and toward Atwood's ranch by Gracious Creek.

By the time they were far enough from Marmot Gulch to slow their pace, Jessie still hadn't said a word. She seemed to be fighting back tears of bitter anger. Holding her torn shirt closed, she showed no embarrassment that the tops of her breasts were exposed; that was just the way it was. Coleson had observed a respectful silence since volunteering to accompany her, and he left conversation up to her, in her own time.

Finally, with sobs breaking her voice, she said, "They were going to kill me, too. Just like that."

Coleson inquired, "What d'you mean, you *too*?"

Angrily she shot back, "Just like all the others, you . . ." Then she realized Coleson didn't know about the massacre. "Where the hell you been? Haven't you heard?"

Coleson shook his head. "Been in Denver. Heard what?"

When Jessie described the atrocity, Coleson was so shaken he had to dismount. He became dizzy and sat on a rock, lowering his head in disbelief. Their mutual stupor and rage became a bond of understanding between them as they again took to the trail.

When they arrived, the Atwood homestead was in mourning over the death of young Darnell. Soon after arriving there the day before, the handsome ranch hand, ashen from blood loss, had turned suddenly cold and fallen into deep shock. The wound across his thigh had slashed his artery, and nothing they could do would stem the bleeding. Not long after Jessie's departure for Redemption, his shallow

124

breathing finally stopped. His unseeing eyes remained half-closed, his chin fell slack, and the valley echoed with his brother's sobs.

Darnell's body lay on a makeshift bier in the high-raftered main room. Arvilla and Rosilda had taken it upon themselves to clean and dress it in a dignified manner. The Bible Atwood had used for a proper reading still lay in the deceased's hands. Arvilla, her face drawn and reddened from steady crying, now sat stoically sullen on the far side of the room, but she could not hold back her tears when Jessie appeared showing evidence of her own dire struggle.

She and Arvilla found some comfort in each other's arms, but there was no hiding their fear. Judge Atwood, feeling awkward in his inability to set everything right, welcomed the tall geologist into his home, while Rosilda saw to Jessie's personal needs and her son tended to Coleson's belongings. A warm meal was begun for the new arrivals.

Atwood hovered about the house in a torpid state, filled with trepidation that reliable help was too far away. Coleson and Ki assumed the responsibility of preparing the homestead for whatever defense they could muster, never admitting aloud just how poor their defense would truly be, although Atwood kept a respectable supply of ammo for every weapon he owned. As he put it, "I've lived long enough to know the value of being well protected." When all was complete—every available firearm loaded, every box of ammunition at hand, every window and door blockaded—the ragged, shocked group went off to their beds to rest for what they were certain would be a long ordeal. All except for Coleson. He was headed out the door when Atwood inquired why.

"Looks like you got a house full, Judge," said the tall blond. "I'll be right there in your barn, if you ain't objecting."

Atwood wouldn't hear of it. Truth was, he felt far safer with Coleson in the house—particularly after Jessie's brief account of Coleson's skilled shooting. The geologist didn't mind sharing the big room with Darnell's corpse, and with his saddlebags and pistol rigs set down on the wide floor planks beside him, he settled down on the high-backed couch for a cramped sleep.

Dawn came gray and shrouded in fog. An eerie stillness clouded the valley. Unable to sleep very comfortably, Jessie padded downstairs to find the main room warm and secure. Through the windows, she could see the mists moving across the fields and past the trees like armies of ghosts slowly retreating before the rising sun. She stepped close to where Coleson slept with his face mostly hidden beneath a heavy woolen blanket. His breathing was deep and slow.

In the open top of his bag lay the .44–40 Merwin Hulbert upon a small sheaf of booklets. They were different than the one she had seen back in town, so she carefully slipped a few from the pile to examine them. Among the group was the familiar *Guide to the Mineral Treasures of the Great Basin* by Cole Johnston. But there were also the *Hand Book to the Gold Fields of the Dakotas* by Chauncey James, "Being a complete guide to the Gold Regions of the Black Hills & Missouri River"; the *Old Prospector's Guide Book to the Hidden Gold of Montezuma* by Shawn C. James; and *The Manual of Forgotten Gold Hills of California* by James E. Shaughnessy. A nervous sensation bubbled through her chest with the unsettling realization that this handsome stranger might be even stranger than she had thought. She crouched to replace the booklets beneath the revolver. The unmistakable sound of a hammer cocking greeted her just inches from her head. Turning slowly to Coleson, she saw the protrusion of something rigid beneath his blanket. His eyes were just barely exposed at the blanket's edge. Jessie showed no fear.

Lifting one book for him to see, she whispered, "So what is it: Cole, John, Chauncey, Shawn, or James?"

The geologist let down the hammer of his Colt and struggled to a sitting position. Jessie stood and dropped the book upon the saddlebag.

"John Coleson's my real name, so far as I can tell."

"What the hell's that supposed to mean?" she replied.

"My mom was widowed when I was just a whelp. Married so many times after, I weren't sure what my real dad's name was." He looked down at his bags. "Far as them books go, they ain't no better'n snake oil tonic. Just something I do real good—for the money is all."

"And I'm supposed to believe you?" she said.

Coleson shrugged. "Ain't supposed to do nothing but what you're capable."

By midday, the sun had burned off the thick fog and brought warmth into the deep valley. Everyone in the house was up, doing very little, it being Sunday. Their eyes frequently cast expectantly about the perimeter of the compound. Jessie was tired of waiting.

With tallow soap, a thick flannel, and some fresh clothing in hand, she was headed down to the creek when she sighted Ki and Will returning to the house. They each carried a shovel and a rifle. When they met, they stood quietly looking into one another's eyes. Ki asked if Jessie was okay and, seeing that she wore her rig, left her to go unattended.

Where Gracious Creek tumbled over some shallows and into a smooth, rock-lined elbow, it was deep enough to swim in. Stepping through the shallows to the other side, Jessie set down her things in a sunny clearing that was partially screened by a stand of reeds and began to undress. Removing the calico shirt she had borrowed from Arvilla, she massaged her abundant breasts. They swayed and bounced as she bent over and pulled off her boots. She peeled her tight-fitting denims from her shapely hips, down her smooth, muscular legs, and stood nude while she tested the water with her toe, the warm sunlight bringing a rich luster to her plush triangle of coppery pubic hair. Squatting down to the water's edge, she slipped in softly and swam to ward off the chill. She returned to the edge by the blind of reeds and washed herself in knee-high water, feeling renewed. She heard a twig snap.

Dropping low into the water, she peered through the reeds to see someone approaching on the far side of the swimming hole. It was Coleson, and he hadn't noticed her. He came to the creek and undressed. Having hesitated to reveal herself sooner, she felt awkward now that he was naked. She merely stared at this fine specimen of male beauty.

A jolt of excitement coursed through her veins upon seeing the short hair that matched the blond locks on his head, and even more because of the handsome appendage that hung between his legs. She folded her arms across her chilled breasts while he turned his back and squatted to place his clothing on the rock, showing off his fit buttocks and pendulous scrotum. He turned toward her to enter the water and still didn't notice her.

She stood still for what seemed an eternity; observing the lean muscles in his arms ripple as he bathed, and imagining the delight of touching him. Soon he was finished, and he started to pull himself out of the water. With his back turned, Jessie thought it a good time to sneak herself out, so gripping the rocks beneath her, she stepped up.

And slipped.

The plop and splash couldn't have been missed, and when the two bathers turned, they feasted their eyes on each other's naked body without the least embarrassment. The warm sun on Coleson's penis made it rise like a flower toward the light, while the cold water in which Jessie had stood so long had made her pink-brown nipples stand erect, casting shadows down the soft curves of her tits. Her parted lips seemed ready to speak, and though no words came forth, her message seemed clear.

Turning once more to lift herself out, she slipped again, and before she knew it, Coleson's voice came from just behind her shoulder.

"Help you up?"

She stood to face him, ready as ever to assert herself, but again words never came.

"Didn't mean to invade your privacy, Jessie . . . but, to be honest, I'm sure glad I did."

Her chest began to heave. When she accepted Coleson's hand, his touch sent bolts of lightning through her. He stepped forward to help her up the embankment, but instead of climbing forward, Jessie merely stood still and let him draw near. Her hand slid up his arm and around his shoulder while he drew his hand around her hourglass waist, and they kissed, tentatively at first, then more deeply, sighing with relief and abandon.

Coleson whispered in a husky voice, "I wouldn't have guessed this could happen, but, lord knows, I wanted it."

Kissing her again, he caressed her bountiful breasts, pulling her nipples toward him gently. His fingertips drew gooseflesh along her spine as he moved them down from the nape of her neck and into the soft crease of her ass. She gasped when he kneaded her butt, spreading her cheeks in anticipation of what was to come.

"Help me up," Jessie sighed.

They spread her clothing across the rock and lay together, clasped tightly.

"Jessie, are you sure about this?"

"The only thing I'm sure about is that we might not be alive tomorrow."

She reached down and stroked Coleson's thick penis to a hard erection, pulling it firmly and slowly. She ran her finger lightly around the bottom of his balls, causing the horny stranger to buck his pelvis.

"And I'm sure," she continued, "that we can start some real fire together."

She lifted a leg and straddled him, never letting go of his cock. Leaning forward, she used the tip of his purple-headed shaft to separate her labia and wiggled and rubbed it across her clitoris, driving them both crazy with lust,

129

Coleson raising his head to suckle and massage her plush breasts. His breathless gasping and writhing pelvis signaled his desire, and circling his cock around the drenching warmth of her open vagina, Jessie lowered herself upon him, raising her knees to receive his full length.

She held him by his shoulders, lifted herself upon her feet, and proceeded to rise and fall upon his ramrod cock and make it glisten with her vaginal fluids. When her knees tired, she set them down and leaned forward to kiss Coleson's mouth. Her breathing was heavy, and her mouth fell away from his to end up by his ear, which received her hot breath and heightening pants of pleasure. She swiveled and bucked her hips wildly upon him, coaxing his penis nearly to explosion. He cast his disbelieving eyes upon her fine figure, clasped to him in unconscious throes of passion, as her round, white ass bounced and her vagina repeatedly swallowed his entire throbbing cock. He planted his heels and bent his knees and began bucking like a bronco, sending his engorged penis home and bringing her to a moaning climax.

"Yes, yes!" she cried as the first orgasm wracked her folded body. She widened her legs and began rubbing her vulva up and down across Coleson's pubic bone, and he could tell by the shivering of her legs that she was approaching yet another, greater climax.

He held fast to the orbs of her ass, stroking and rubbing them, separating and pushing them together. He slipped one hand down to where their sexes were joined and explored her thick, wet lips and moistened hair. He slipped one, then two fingers into her, alongside his penis, dousing them in Jessie's sweet, copious flow, feeling her fluids run freely down his scrotum. He withdrew his saturated fingers and drew them lightly upward, across the sensitive pucker of her anus and up toward her spine. Her sudden groan of passion was all the signal he required, and he returned his moistened hand downward. Drawing delicate circles, he teased and titillated her butthole and could feel her trying to push down

130

upon his hand and penis together, full of want and hunger. The excitement mounted within him as well, and placing the pad of one finger upon her hot little bung, he pressed and wiggled and rammed his erupting cock as deep as possible. Jessie's legs flexed against his, and lifting herself upon her arms, she bucked harder than ever, driving Coleson's finger in to the first knuckle and triggering blinding simultaneous orgasms in them, with convulsive tremors that took minutes to subside.

Jessie collapsed where she lay and wiped her mouth like someone recovering from madness. Coleson chuckled when she flexed her vaginal muscles and tickled his sensitive flesh as she squeezed him out. She looked at him with a wide smile and half-closed eyes.

"You know, Mister Whatever Your Name Is," Jessie panted, "when I saw the way you handle a gun, I was impressed. But now I see it's all in the trigger finger. And the way you handle that cannon of yours! I think I'd like to take regular lessons."

"Don't know who's gonna be teaching who, Jess, but it's a safe bet I'll be comin' back to this school."

They lay still for a moment, enjoying their exhaustion in the sun. Jessie nestled her head upon Coleson's shoulder.

"I feel safe with you, John. And don't ask me why. Isn't that foolish?"

It was a question that went unanswered.

They slept awhile. And when Coleson awoke to the sounds of birdcalls in the breeze, he found himself wanting this enticing young beauty once again. They lay nested like spoons, and his renewed erection pressed against the warm softness of her plush bottom. Wetting his fingers in his mouth, he gently slid one hand between her legs and moistened her vulva once again. He guided his lusty rod into Jessie's welcoming sex and then eased himself in and out, excited by the sight of her soft buttocks against his abdomen. Jessie groaned in her partial wakefulness and thrust back her ass for better penetration. Soon Coleson expended himself inside her once more, his hands wrapped securely around her trim tummy and his face in her sweet-smelling hair.

They bathed in the swimming hole again, and while dressing, they heard the ranch-house bell tolling calmly.

"We'd best get back," Jessie surmised. "Time to pay respects."

★

Chapter 11

"With all respect to Will and his brother," Jessie announced, "I can't sit here doing nothing about all this. We gotta have a plan."

Ki voiced his agreement, but no one seemed to know where all this was headed. Life for the time being had become reduced to satisfying immediate needs: giving Darnell a proper burial, staying alert and ready in case Benton should attempt a bushwhacking, preparing meals no one really had any appetite for. Everyone stayed close to the house, and the mining operations across the ridge stood dormant on this day of rest. Even the funeral was a hurried affair for which the judge provided a reading. They all nervously peered over their shoulders, anticipating trouble—everyone but Will, who let the dirt sift slowly through his fingers onto the shrouded corpse, then bent for another handful twice more before Rosilda took him gently by the shoulders and led him away from the grave. Ki and Coleson closed the hole. It seemed the sun dropped out of the sky early that day. Not long after the last glimmer of daylight bequeathed the heavens to the stars, the beleaguered folks immersed themselves in discussing their plight.

"The first telegraph I dispatched to Fort Steele was answered," Jessie said, "but Colonel Bobbitt—he's a good friend of mine—was out on maneuvers. The telegraph I dispatched yesterday was marked urgent, but who knows when help will get here—*if* it gets here."

"I say we get every armed man in the company together and go in there tomorrow and have it out with 'em," Arvilla stated. "An eye for an eye."

"That amounts to all-out war," Judge Atwood responded. "What would that accomplish but more innocent dead? They would retaliate until every last one of us is killed."

"And," Ki interjected, "your mines, your mills, everything would be absorbed."

Sitting in his despondency on the far side of the timber-raftered room, young Will broke his silence.

"They killed everyone, not just my brother! That bastard Ryde Benton deserves to die eighteen times over, and you're all gettin' shiney butts, yammerin' about what you should or shouldn't do! Well, I'm telling you right now. That son of a bitch is going to die, and I swear, I ain't gonna rest until he does. I aim to see that polecat go down hard, and I'm gonna do it first chance, just like Darnell woulda. I swear . . ."

The boy fell into sobs that quieted the household and sent Rosilda away crying. All the talk of revenge coming from the younger folks frightened the old judge, who had spent a career trying to replace mob law with the law of juries and upright folks who wanted less bloodshed, not more. He suggested they let the proper authorities bring Benton and his cohorts to justice, which elicited polite but firm disagreement from Arvilla.

Sitting in a large rocker beside Atwood's Winchester, which leaned against the wall, Coleson had listened quietly to the discussion while cleaning his .44–40. But now he found something to say.

"Ryde Benton ain't nothin'."

All heads turned. They weren't prepared to have their

134

anger diverted. Coleson continued to clean his pistol as he spoke.

"Y'all talkin' about Benton, and sure as I'm setting here now, him and his back-shootin' varmints deserve to die slow and painful. But the man who really deserves to eat some lead is that snake-eyed pantywaist up there on the hill. Padgett."

"We all know he can't be trusted," blustered the judge, "but are you saying that he's responsible for murder?"

"I am. I just know it," answered Coleson. "Benton's a cross-eyed *pistolero*, a back-stabber. Padgett uses him to back his play, is all. No, sir, Padgett's the head of it all. Cut him off, the rest'll die."

Although Arvilla and the judge spoke simultaneously, Jessie and Ki's interest was piqued by what the tall blond seemed to know and wasn't telling.

Jessie said, "Are you saying that Padgett was behind the entire massacre?"

Coleson nodded once. "You said yourself, the meetin' was his idea. 'Sides, that poisoned meat, that's as sure a sign as I can figure, it was ol' Padgett behind it."

"He's done this before?"

Coleson's nod was subtle. "Oh, yeah."

"Mr. Coleson," said Atwood, "you need not be so cryptic. What is it you're saying?"

"What I'm saying is this: Poison's just as good as Padgett's signature. He don't have the nerve nor the know-how for throwing down against another in a gun-fight, so he finds these hardscrabble misfits like Benton and them 'Redeemed' folks to bring things to a showdown. I seen it before. I been on Padgett's tail a might too long to be wrong."

Atwood considered a moment. "There a price on Padgett's head, Coleson? Hmm? You hunting bounty?"

Coleson looked through his gun barrel and just shook his head.

"Ain't no price ridin' on that no-account turd I know

of. Fact, too many folks think he's an upstanding pillar of the community." He clicked his tongue. "He ain't worth no bounty. Hell, I'll kill him for free. That ol' boy's lower than a sidewinder and deserves to die like one."

Arvilla snidely remarked, "Reckon you don't care much for the man."

Ki asked, "So how do you know so much about him?"

The handsome stranger snapped shut the cylinder of the pistol and raised his eyes.

"He's my stepfather."

Virgil Nettles was hating himself. When he awoke that Sunday morning and heard the single bell of Marmot Gulch Baptist Church ringing in the few believers among the Redeemed, his hand fell away from the half-empty flask on a shelf above his cot. He didn't want that searing fire in his throat that only got worse with age, not better. He did, however, want that flood of warmth and calm that spread down his chest and into his limbs with every swallow, that welcome relief, that bit of disregard for everyone but himself. He didn't want to be haunted anymore, as he had been every Sunday morning for nearly fifteen years, by images of former Sundays when a certain petite and popular woman who shared his name and gave birth to his daughter walked with him to church amid the peal of bells and the bustle of busy Colorado Springs. He did want to turn his mind away from those images forever, not so much to forget them as to avoid the pain they caused. The easiest, most habitual way was by losing himself to the evil spirits of the bottle.

For the first time in his life, he admitted to himself he was a whiskey soak.

He couldn't deny how unhappy he was, how worthless his life had become since his younger days as a lawman on the Front Range. About the only time he could admit that to himself was before the day's drinking had begun. Nothing mattered much anymore, not even beautiful Lydia, who'd cast a blind eye to him immediately after her brief,

136

seductive attentions, so he might as well drink. His unhappiness must have driven him to her, just as it drove him to the ugly old seer, Madame Rena, who lived behind the St. Ives Saloon. She specialized in curing "diseases of the heart" but only laughed at him when he thundered out of her tassle-hung apartment because she had lied about Lydia's true feelings of affection for the marshal, revealed to her through "the crystal's all-seeing eye."

He hated himself more for letting Benton intimidate him and bribe him with his nemesis, whiskey. But mostly, he hated himself for not helping the lovely Starbuck woman. His self-loathing stuck in his throat like a bone when, late that afternoon, he passed by the Lodgepole and saw the posse gathering.

Brazenly, Benton's cronies made no attempt at discretion as they holstered rifles upon their saddles and tied around their necks bandannas meant to cover their faces. Many of them were drinking, and amid their raucous shouts and cackling laughter, Nettles could hear glass breaking. Any self-respecting marshal would have busted in and run the coyotes off, and for the first time in a long while, Nettles had a mind to do so.

The door of the Lodgepole swung wide, and Nettles saw the unmistakable figure of Ryde Benton emerge, casting a long shadow in the angling light. He didn't stand long, and with a final round of loud whoops, the posse galloped off into the darkness of Marmot Gulch, without Benton, to Nettles's surprise.

Nettles was confused: He knew what he should do, but his feet were not cooperating. He became afraid, not for himself, but for the two young ladies who had become embroiled in this very deadly war, and all at once he found himself walking away from the Lodgepole Saloon, back up the main road, past the newspaper building, and into the Touchstone.

"Hey, Kentucky," greeted the ruddy-faced barkeep. "What'll it be?"

"Nothin' jest now," Nettles answered, surprising himself. He had come hoping Lydia could tell him something, about where Benton's men were headed to, but she was nowhere to be seen. The sun was already bloodying itself on the hogbacks before he started back to his cramped, smelly office. Since he'd had no hard drink all day long, his hands trembled.

Lamplight from his office spilled out the open door and onto the rutted roadway. He paused. His eyes drifted to the tidy little sign above the lintel that read, "Town Marshal, Redemption, Col." Although he had been marshal here for over ten years, he thought it fitting that his name didn't appear on the sign. As far as upholding the law went, Nettles knew he might as well have been invisible.

But no more. He swore he'd change all that.

Standing beside his file cabinet, he stared at the guns in the rack. He stooped over and opened a low drawer, pulling out an old gunbelt that was folded in all the wrong places. Throwing it to his desk, he went to the key cabinet, chose a small key on a ring, and wiggled it into the lock, holding the chain that secured his pistols. The chain coming out of the trigger guards made a rasping buzz. His hand hovered over the pistols indecisively.

He grabbed the Remington No. 3 and fondled it a moment, getting reacquainted with its balance and weight. It had been a long time. He threw open the cylinder and, raising the gun to the light, peered down the filthy barrel. Replacing it on the rack, he picked up the Remington-Rider, a handsome iron with fluted cylinder. Not many were seen in these parts. He was about to check the chambers, but then he wondered whether he had the correct cartridges.

Putting the pistol back on the rack, he began rummaging through his vast disarray, turning up keys and rowels of spurs, old bread crusts and various tools he had stopped wondering about long ago. He found a cartridge box marked .44–100 center fire. "That's the Number Three," he muttered and opened the box. It was filled with dice.

On top of a small crate within arm's reach of the jail cell were several other boxes, and rifling two of them, he found one filled with good .45 cartridges. He selected the Peacemaker with the nicked grip. He sighed with a slight shake of the head as he recalled the last time he had used the battered old Colt—in making the arrest that destroyed his courage, his career, and his family. Maybe it would be different this time, he thought. "Couldn't git no worse."

He sat behind his cluttered desk and commenced cleaning the weapon. When he was satisfied it was as clean as he could get it, he loaded it and slipped a dozen cartridges into his gunbelt loops. He had entirely missed the paper Coleson had hidden in the Remington-Rider.

"Turn down that lamp, would you, Jessie?" Coleson asked while peering out the window.

It was too dark outside to see anything with the room lit. All the other lamps in the house had been doused for safety.

As she lowered the wick on the wall sconce, Jessie said, "When I spoke with Padgett, he mentioned he had been married once. Was she your mom?"

"Yep."

"He said she passed on of a . . . some kinda wasting disease."

Coleson exhaled loudly, still facing the glass.

" 'Wastin' disease,' my butt. Yeah, she wasted away, all right, but it weren't no disease."

"I'm sorry," Jessie said quietly.

The tall stranger remained silent. He turned away from the window and with a sigh set himself down on a thick easy chair, standing a rifle against its arm.

"What kind of service are you in?" she asked. She caught his eye. "The swivels on your pistols. They look military."

With a slight shake of the head, he replied, "Used to ride for Fargo 'n' Comp'ny."

Just then, Ki walked into the room and announced, "Animals are all stabled, and every door from the kitchen back to the springhouse is barred tight. I'll be in the back."

Jessie thanked him and turned back to Coleson. "You're not with them anymore? What happened?"

"Nothing happened. They just didn't like my methods." He gave the distinct impression that he didn't want to talk about that particular issue. When Jessie complimented his marksmanship, he modestly tried not to smile. Her curiosity about where he had learned to shoot so well was rewarded with still another colorful stroke to this man's portrait: Before working for Wells Fargo, he had worked as a market hunter for mining operations up and down the Front Range. His story was suspect, like everything else about the guy. He looked much too young to have been a market hunter before the big trail drives took over. More than likely, his time spent roaming the mountain chains had been in search of his vanished stepfather. A hunt for vengeance. Still, he claimed it was the trail drives that drove him into other lines of work.

"Every gun-totin' cowpunch I knew who was his own man up this way was put outta work. But then, that's progress, I reckon."

From upstairs, Arvilla's voice rose from an alarmed call to a desperate shout, "Jessie! I hear horses! Jessie!"

The sitting-room window exploded into a hail of glass shards, and curtains billowed inward as the fusillade began, sending Jessie and Coleson to the floor. Bullets peppered the rear walls, splinters flew, and curtains danced to the ping and knock of the marauders' deadly music.

"Ki!" Jessie yelled, only to be answered by Coleson insisting she stay down. "Ki, they're coming around from your left!" she cried.

The barrage went unbroken from the front of the house, preventing Jessie and Coleson from returning fire, but from the bedroom above, Arvilla's angry, growling voice could just be heard between shots she carefully fired from the

140

judge's Winchester. At one point, she cursed the darkness aloud then resumed firing as she spied the ghost like figures whisking through the night.

The mounted gunmen circled the house, and with the sound of shattering glass came Rosilda's fearful screaming from her bedroom. Upon hearing her cries, her boy, thinking she was hit, came rushing toward her. But being careless about staying low before the window, he caught a slug in the side of his chest that flung him across the room. Bloodcurdling screams filled the house as Rosilda held the stunned, wide-eyed boy in her lap, helplessly clutching him to her blood-soaked breast.

In burst Arvilla. Seeing what had happened, she dropped below the window and pulled a solid-backed chair in front of herself. Aiming between it and the wall, she dropped her first gunman, with a burning bullet through his skull. It became a game of duck-hunting, trying to lead fast-moving targets in poor visibility. She wished she were firing a shotgun instead.

Gunfire erupted at the back of the house and was returned by Ki through rosette-shaped cutouts in the kitchen's window shutters. Amid the stuttering gunfire, he could hear wild neighing from the stables and the clamor of panicked hooves. Ki fired several shots from one position and upon reloading, assumed a new vantage point as the bulk of desperadoes moved past. When he had managed to drop two horses from under their riders, he brought down one of the gunmen, who was firing back from behind his stricken animal. Having pumped two shots into the exposed part of the saddle closest to his mark, Ki quickly changed positions to gain a different angle. From there, he leveled his sights upon the side of the crouching man's head, and with two squeezes of the trigger in rapid succession, he silenced the man's guns for good.

While Jessie and Coleson held their own in the front room, firing in tandem and reloading expertly, Judge Atwood and young Will, too, were causing considerable

141

damage from a ground-floor room adjacent to the kitchen. Resting the devastating Sharps "Big Fifty" on the sill of a well-protected window, Atwood chose his targets carefully, aimed patiently, and with each cannonlike blast, dropped a horse and rider hard to the sod. With his own self-cocking revolver, Will would then pick off the rider as he struggled to his feet.

Sitting beneath a window with her back to the wall, Jessie paused from reloading. She noticed that something had changed.

"Listen!" she said to Coleson. "They're stopping."

Coleson leaned on his elbow, gunsmoke wafting from the barrel of his Merwin Hulbert. Arvilla's Winchester was firing more frequently than anything outside. They could hear the echoes of the reports travel up the long valley. Atwood appeared in the archway at the back of the room, kneeling.

"Do you hear?" he asked with surprise. "They've stopped. Have we beat them? Have we?"

"Prob'ly regrouping," Coleson replied. "Maybe gatherin' weapons off the ground. Just stay low."

"We've got to stop this!" hissed Atwood. "This is madness!"

He rushed to the door, and young Will followed hesitantly. Coleson tried to block his way.

"Where in hell you goin', Judge? You wanna git killed?"

"I'm going to talk to them. Can't you see we've beaten them? They've probably run off by now."

For the first time, Coleson recognized the distracted look in the old man's eyes. The timber of reason had snapped like a twig, and Coleson was ready to use force to keep him back, when suddenly Arvilla called from Rosilda's room.

"Where'd they go? Jessie? You see 'em? I think I saw 'em get gone!"

"You see?" Atwood blurted. "You see? We've beaten them back."

He pulled the bar from the door and tried to open it, but

142

Coleson clamped down on his wrist urgently, "Judge! You don't know what you're doing!"

Atwood stared into Coleson's eyes sternly, and his voice was cold and calm.

"Look here, son. This here's my house you're in, and this is my land, and my life. There are dead and wounded lying out there, and I will not tolerate any more. You will release my hand. I only want to speak to them through the door. I assure you, I do not want to die."

Will crouched nearby with his revolver in his shaking hand. He was scared almost breathless.

"Don't do it, Judge," he pleaded. "Don't."

Jessie yelled from across the room, "These people aren't just going to disappear, Judge, and they aren't going to reason with you!"

Nonetheless, Atwood pulled his arm from Coleson's clutch and threw the latch. Everyone but Will ducked.

"Hey!" yelled Atwood. "We've had enough and you have, too! You hear?" Only the chill Colorado night was listening. "I am a former judge of Rio Blanco County. I am unarmed. Are you out there?" He opened the door slightly wider and could neither hear nor see anything. "We can settle this with Padgett peacefully. Listen! This is not worth all the gold in the Rockies to me. If it's the damned mines you want, we can work something out. Do you hear me?"

With that, he swung the door wide, and before he uttered another syllable, a bright flash exploded before him, the large-caliber slug grazing his head and throwing him backward on top of young Will, whose pistol hand was pinned beneath. A barrage of gunfire erupted once more, and bullets whirred over Coleson's head as he crouched for cover.

Struggling to get out from under Atwood's body, Will blanched upon seeing towering above him just outside the door a masked rider, laughing loudly. The marauder raised his pistol to end Will's life. The boy's gun hand came free. He pointed and fired three frenzied times, the first bullet

143

shattering the rider's face, the next two firing high with the recoil. He kicked the door hard against Atwood's feet, and it slammed just as the rider crashed to the porch floor beneath his horse.

Having run to a front room during the lull, Arvilla resumed her defense there and continued until it seemed most of the gunmen had moved around the building. Running to the far side, she found a place to make a stand, but hesitated firing when she saw an eerie orange light illuminate the grounds.

They were torching the house.

No sooner had it dawned on her than Ki began yelling from downstairs, "Fire! Fire in the house!"

Bullets continued to buzz through the windows. Jessie moved toward the back of the house to help Ki. Behind her came a bottle flying through the gaping window, and when it hit the floor, it exploded into a raging curtain of fire that clung to the floor and the furniture.

Everyone scrambled. Will lifted the dazed judge to his knees, and Coleson was cut off from them by the flames. Another bottle crashed, and a new conflagration erupted across the room, leaving the boy and the old man only one exit. Shaking the judge violently, Will lifted him to his feet, and cocking his pistol, he yelled to Coleson, "We're gonna run for it!"

Coleson was trapped beside the fireplace, facing a wall of searing flame. His urgings that Will not exit the front went unheard. As soon as he saw the door open and the two of them bolt, his thoughts turned to saving himself.

He holstered his two pistols and snapped the leather flaps down over them. Backing up as far across the room as the flames would allow, he lurched two long strides toward the burning couch and, planting one foot on its back, catapulted himself upward to hang from a rafter. His grasp on the large, smooth timber was tenuous at best, and he fought to hook his elbow around it with feet kicking wildly. The rising heat reddened his skin, and the updraft lifted his hair. He could barely keep his eyes open in the boiling radiance.

A brief volley of gunfire out front took on a more sickening affect when Coleson heard perverse laughter over the roar of the flames. He listened as additional sporadic discharges spoke of the gruesome mutilation of the old judge and brave young Will, who died a man.

He swung his legs to try to catch the next rafter, but couldn't keep the sole of his boot upon it. The span was just beyond his reach. Shimmying out over the center of the inferno, he came to a crossbrace and used it to pull himself atop the beam. He had to do something quick, and he couldn't go back. The flames consuming the couch were already blackening the logs high up the wall. He held tightly to the crossbrace and stood precariously in leather-soled boots.

He figured he could leap to the next rafter, and if he could hit the crossbrace chest-first, he would be almost home. From there, it was a long leap to the other side of the conflagration, just this side of the archway. His only escape.

He planted his heels forward on the timber. He leaned over. With arms swinging, he leapt and flew—and slammed into the next brace with his shoulder, hugging it for dear life. Again he clambered to a standing position, nearly exhausted. Every breath was deathly painful as the smoke grew thicker and blacker. Again he planted his heels and leaned. Using his arms like a double pendulum, he drew them back and swung them forward.

And slipped.

As he led with one foot, his thrusting rear foot lost its hold and his jump wasn't nearly far enough. His forearms and palms slapped the face of the wide beam, causing his body to swing forward before he lost his grip. He yelped involuntarily as he fell, crashing to the floor with a jarring impact that he thought dislocated his shoulder. Utterly dazed, he felt nauseated by the smell of blood in his nose and lost track of how long he lay there, near the creeping flame's edge, unsure whether it was the fire or his bones that were burning.

In the kitchen, Ki had ceased firing when Jessie arrived. His only thought was to bring her to safety. He tossed her his gun, saying, "Cover me!" and threw open the back door communicating to the springhouse passageway. He came right back and shouted, "This way, through the stables!"

Just then they heard Coleson's wail and his devastating crash. Jessie ran to him and, pulling his good arm over her shoulders, helped him to his feet, yelling, "Arvilla! Rosy! Get out! *Now!*" She struggled to the back of the building, practically dragging the groggy Coleson.

Arvilla didn't have to be told to flee a burning house, but Rosilda did. The horrified mother clung to her son in agony, oblivious to the growing peril. The feisty Jessup girl was unable to pull her from her child. It only made matters worse when Arvilla shouted, "Leave him! Save yourself!" For Rosilda would rather have died there, too, than to outlive her only child. Finally Arvilla grabbed the boy's ankles and began sliding him from the room, challenging Rosilda to a bizarre tug of war.

"Jessie!" cried Arvilla, still clutching her rifle. "Rosy won't come!" She ran back to her room and threw a shoulder bag on. She dropped a couple of cartridge boxes into it and ran back to Rosilda, calling, "Jessie, come quick!"

Coleson tottered on his feet when Jessie left him to help her old schoolmate. Entering the main room, she cowered before the intense heat and realized the roof was already in danger of collapse.

"She won't leave him," Arvilla gasped.

Jessie fell to her knees and held Rosilda by the shoulders and patted her face.

"Rosy, we don't have much time. I'll carry your boy for you, but you've got to come."

She pleaded with her while trying to lift the boy, and soon Rosilda's grip weakened and Jessie was leading them

146

downstairs. In the kitchen, she found the two men soaking blankets in the springhouse trough.

"Wrap one of these around each of you!" Ki shouted.

Jessie passed the dead boy back to his mother, who plopped absently into the first chair she saw, next to a bullet-ridden shuttered window. Before Jessie could hand over the sopping blanket Ki had thrown her, a single gunshot rang out. Jessie and Arvilla gaped in stunned horror as Rosilda slumped over her son's limp body, a thick rivulet of blood flowing from behind her ear and down her chin.

★

Chapter 12

Another incendiary exploded against the side of a shattered window, raining burning fluid into the kitchen and causing Jessie and Arvilla to leap into the springhouse passage. In moments the entire room was engulfed as the flame grew, consuming everything like an immense, deep-voiced monster. Pulling an icy-cold blanket around her shoulders, Jessie ran through the tack room and into the stables beyond, to find Coleson had already saddled three horses and was readying a fourth. Ki quickly wrapped blankets around the heads of the spooked creatures and yelled for the women to mount.

Bursts of hungry fire erupted across the outside of the stables, and through the slats they could see the orange menace crawling up the walls.

"Quick! They're torching the walls!" shouted Coleson. He raced back to the springhouse, which was already covered with orange-and-blue tentacles of fire. Emerging with a bucket of water, he doused the horses and riders and, wrapping a wet blanket about himself, leapt onto his proud Appaloosa. The springhouse roof buckled and fell. "Follow me!" he cried.

With a few pats on the animal's neck, Coleson suddenly kicked hard and propelled the large-chested animal straight against the wall. With a yell, he pulled the beast into a leap that cleared a trough and sent the animal crashing through the sheets of flame hooves-first, while the women followed close behind in a dazzling shower of bright cinders, sparking orange against the dark night. The incredible sight frightened their attackers, and shouting voices came out of the darkness.

Bringing up the rear on a responsive dun mare, Ki kept low to its neck, hell-bent on staying as close to the others as possible. But several of the gunslingers were ready for him, having missed their shots at Coleson and the women. Ki had barely cleared the building and begun removing the blanket from the mare's head when the first of several bullets whizzed past him. Taking an old model Smith & Wesson Russian from his belt and keeping one foot planted in the stirrup, he threw a leg over the cantle and held fast to the horn. The Russian's short, blued barrel belched three .44-caliber slugs at the shadowy figures riding toward him, but nothing did much good.

A large-caliber discharge flashed. The concussion knocked the screaming animal down, and would have crushed Ki underneath had he not moved so quickly. When he hit the ground, his foot was caught momentarily beneath the saddle skirt as the killers approached. One of the riders leapt to the ground gloating and cocked his pistol, but Ki dropped him with some burning lead in the chest. Cocking the gun again, he withdrew a *shuriken* from his vest and snapped it off at his next attacker, who never saw it coming. The razor-sharp throwing star whirred orange in the firelight and sliced into the unsuspecting raider's throat, dumping him over the croup of his mount as Ki freed his foot.

Looking over her shoulder at full gallop, Arvilla realized Ki was no longer behind her. Reining in her rambunctious stallion and dropping the wet blanket, she veered sharply around, but she reined her mount too high. The peppery-tempered animal reared, nearly throwing her, but regaining control, she roweled the horse feverishly toward Ki. Sitting high in the saddle, she leveled the Winchester, fearing she had lost too much time.

Coming out of the apocalyptic darkness, she wasn't recognized by the killers until it was too late. She levered off three shots, bringing down one man and maiming the horses of two others. Having whisked past them, she circled back and gave the two fallen riders a taste of lead they would never live to tell about, blasting them square in their faces.

"Ki!" she called. "Behind you!"

Spinning on his heels and dropping low at the same time, Ki was saved from catching a bullet in the back and fanned off two shots at one oncoming marauder, raising two puffs of blood from his chest and knocking him backward off his mount to land crushingly upon the base of his spine. Arvilla levered off a flurry of hot lead at another rider, whose return fire was rendered useless when his good arm was shattered.

In a flash, Arvilla circled back once more, calling out Ki's name as she came. The agile samurai readied himself. Putting out his arms toward his oncoming rescuer, he clutched Arvilla's saddle and threw one leg high over the animal's loins, fighting with all his might to hang on while struggling to a sitting position. Gunfire echoed from behind them, and keeping low, Arvilla drove the stallion zigzagging out of range. Soon, even the most rabid among their pursuers gave up. They rejoined their surviving cohorts to watch the Atwood homestead collapse and to pillage the remaining buildings.

Jessie and the others didn't stop running for miles. When they reached the far rise of the valley, Arvilla, who knew the area best, led them into the hills and away from routes of travel. It seemed like a repetition of their flight only two days earlier, but this time they had no place to go.

They traveled high along a wooded ridge until exhaustion made them bivouac in a gravelly clearing amid a copse of aspens. There were two large blankets rolled one each behind Coleson's and Jessie's saddles, still fairly dry, so they paired off—Jessie and Coleson, Ki and Arvilla—to huddle within them while two other blankets were hung in a tree to dry.

The question loomed before them: What now? Jessie felt certain that it would take a lot more firepower to confront the Redemption killers effectively, and Arvilla suggested riding out to Fort Steele. The journey of more than two hundred miles didn't appeal to anyone. Chances were good that the hills were crawling with the Redeemed and the fort would never be reached alive. Denver seemed a better alternative, but that meant passing again straight through Gore country.

"There's got to be somebody honest in Silver Plume or Georgetown," Arvilla whined.

Her exhaustion was destroying her morale. She was perpetually on the verge of tears with the suspicion that Benton and his gang would be flushing them out, closing in on them with each more violent raid. Hope was slipping through her fingers. Apparently it was the four of them against an entire town of cutthroats.

Coleson glanced at Jessie and mumbled that Denver was possible if they were careful—and very lucky. But Jessie also understood that he was saying so only to allay Arvilla's fears and give the impression that they had a real plan. Jessie's stomach was in knots knowing they didn't.

"We'd best get some shut-eye," suggested Coleson. "We got some hard days ahead." Ki volunteered keeping watch, and Coleson thought it a good idea. "Wake me in two or three hours, would ya? You'll need some rest, too."

Jessie offered Coleson the entire blanket and bedded down with Arvilla. She watched Ki with admiration as he sat up in the dark, checking his pistol and the slender curved blade of the *tanto* he always carried in its lacquered sheath, tucked into the waistband of his trousers. He also took inventory of the throwing stars concealed within the inner pockets of his scuffed leather vest. The art of using them, *shuriken-jutsu*, he had mastered long ago, before coming into Jessie's life. He never used them carelessly.

She glanced over at Coleson, who sat on the blanket, calmly loading his two revolvers. Their eyes met, and the subtle turn of Coleson's lip gave Jessie a feeling of assurance and trust. She lay back and made herself comfortable. Above her, the brilliant star-studded sky was slowly clouding over; so, too, her bright-shining eyes, as sleep stole over her and put her worries at bay for the meantime.

The chill of the early morning hours caused the sleeping fugitives to snuggle deep beneath their blankets. Soon the strengthening sun coaxed them out again. As the hue of the sky grew a deeper blue, the mountaintops were dwarfed by mountainous billows of cotton-white clouds above. Exhausted, the fleeing party slept in and missed the change occurring around them. Deep peals of thunder rolled through the valleys from some unseen, distant place, frightening Jessie awake. She leaned upon her elbow and, squinting in the sunlight, was startled to find Coleson and Ki missing.

She leapt to her feet and walked to the clearing's edge to scan the hillsides. One of the horses was gone, but all of the blankets remained. A twig snapped behind her. In one move, she drew and cocked her Colt and spun, ready to fire. Ki walked quietly toward her with one palm raised.

"He's gone," he said. His voice stirred Arvilla from her rest. "Must have slipped out after my watch while I nodded. I can't believe I didn't hear him."

Jessie sensed his disappointment. Owning up to her own lack of awareness still wouldn't assuage his feeling of failure. Just a matter of exhaustion, really. She knew how much he expected of himself. He had spoken to her often in the past of *haragei*, the "gut sense" to which he endlessly strived to open himself, and though she believed Ki possessed a far-advanced gut sense, it would do no good to remind him of it.

"Where do you think he'd go?" Arvilla asked when she was on her feet.

Looking out upon the magnificent mountain scenery, Ki responded, "Only one place now."

Jessie picked up a blanket and walked toward the horses, completing Ki's thought: "Goddamn Redemption."

The posse's trail leading toward Gracious Creek was easy enough to follow, even for a dull-sighted, out-of-practice old coot like Virge Nettles. Every so often he'd find a discarded whiskey bottle or tobacco pouch. He reined in his swaybacked gelding at one point to take a closer look at a dead jackrabbit beneath a sage. A pity and a waste. The poor animal had been riddled with bullets. Don't take that much to kill a hare, he thought. It left little doubt that Benton's friends had come this way.

He stopped to water his sweating horse, a parrot-mouthed old boy with a blaze down his face and badly sloped pasterns, and sat himself beneath a piñon. No matter how much he wiped his neck, nothing seemed to stop him from sweating either, it was so humid. He held his hand out before him. The trembling was getting steadily worse. He wanted a drink something fierce. He pulled on his face and took a deep breath, threw his head back with eyes closed. Finally he grunted to his feet and rummaged through his saddlebags. Pulled out an apple and bit into it with a snap. He removed his canteen and chewed, staring at the fruit as if it were poison, but took another bite anyway, then plopped back down beneath the tree. He wondered apprehensively about what he'd find at Atwood's ranch—it behooved him as marshal to find out. The rowdies had apparently returned to Redemption during the night, if the number of horses

153

around the Lodgepole and in the wagon yard were any indication.

He took a swig of water from the canteen, then another, turning his dry lips inward to wet them, letting liquid spill down his chin. He wet his bandanna and wiped his neck and brow.

Thinking about the Starbuck girl and Arvilla Jessup, he muttered, "Wouldn't mess with neither of'm." He bit the apple. "Hellions," he garbled with his mouth full. Truthfully, he couldn't believe they'd be any match for Benton's crew. With his next bite, he got a mouthful of seeds and spit them out. He chucked the remains and raised the canteen one more time, but sickened by plain water, he recapped it and climbed back into the saddle.

It seemed a long while listening to the rhythmic creak of saddle leather before he rounded the mouth of the valley and saw the thin veil of gray smoke. As the road curved into the wide, flat spread, his heart fluttered. He had been out to the place a handful of times and recognized it. What had once been a group of handsome buildings was now a black skeleton bare to the sky. With the shift of the wind, the smell of fire seared his nostrils.

The enormity of the carnage was like his old wartime nightmares. Men and horses lay scattered about the scorched earth wearing the pained expression they wore at the moment their spirits fled. Inside the gate, over the front drive lay the old judge and a young man, bullet-riddled and powder-burned. Both of Atwood's eyes had been shot out. Closer to the house was Big Dave the Dog-eater lying crumpled, a neat black-and-red hole between his ear and eye. A couple of the fallen horses weren't even dead yet. Their labored breathing and wild eyes were a sight that would stay with Nettles in his dreams. He put them out of their misery with a bullet each. He quickly reloaded the spent chambers.

Everything was gone but an outhouse—the barn, the stables, everything. He nudged the gelding around the wreckage. The glint of steel upon one of the bodies caught his

154

eye. On investigation it appeared to be nothing he had ever seen before—Ki's *shuriken,* still embedded in the saddle scum's throat, right in the artery. The ground was saturated with blood to a radius of nearly a yard. The roof over the spring trough was collapsed, and looking down into the ruins, he saw the legs of a boy under the pile of rubble. The kid looked about as scorched as everything on top of him, leaving Nettles with a queasy feeling in his throat. The stables stunk of burnt flesh, an odor Nettles recalled too clearly from the war. It was a smell you could never entirely shake.

It was a lonely place that made the marshal uneasy. The silence was broken only by the rasping of crows. He counted about a dozen dead—he wasn't interested in being precise with a body count so high. It was war all over again. His hands were trembling more violently now, so he retrieved a small flask from the top of his saddlebag and took a couple of jolts. In a moment, he felt calmer.

A dribble of raindrops on his face warned him of a coming shower which, upvalley, had already begun as a gray smear between earth and sky. Donning his oilcloth poncho, he started the long ride back to Redemption sickened by what he had seen, but galvanized to his purpose: to stand up against that bushwhacking cuss Benton, once and for all.

For Jessie, Ki, and Arvilla, it was agonizingly slow going. Traveling with extreme caution every step of the way was tedious enough, but with two horses among them, at least one person's ass was mighty sore at all times. For much of the way, Jessie rode behind Arvilla, giving the willful Jessup freedom to handle the Winchester. After each rest, seating was juggled, until it came Ki's turn to assume the rear position. It somehow seemed more inappropriate to sit behind Jessie than behind the feisty young beauty whose eyes seemed brighter than usual when looking at Ki. So perching himself atop the cantle, Ki slid into the seat with the small-bottomed girl and took the opportunity to fill his nostrils with her scent.

Whether Jessie intentionally took the lead or Arvilla purposely lagged behind, Ki didn't care. But lag they did, making conversation more relaxed. Just what Ki needed. What was most on his mind was the mindless erection he got from falling against Arvilla's backside and the constant rocking of the animal. On the one hand, he hoped she wouldn't notice. On the other, well . . .

"I'm not crushing you, am I?" he asked. He didn't know Arvilla was smiling.

"I was about to ask you that same question," she replied. "You wearin' your holster in front of you?"

The long pause signaled Ki's surprise.

When she felt him sit up higher, she said, "I didn't mean stop, Ki. That there is the pleasingest feeling I've had in months. I hope you don't figure me impolite for saying so."

Ki couldn't have wished for her to say anything else. A lustful fire ignited in his loins, and he let the swaying of the horse rock him back down against her firm bottom. Suddenly she scooted forward, putting the horn almost flush against her crotch, making more room for Ki to settle in lower.

"I'm considerable attracted to you, Ki," she said, turning her head. "I could think of better times to meet."

"I'm nigh half-crazed for you, Arvilla. Have been since a long time."

"Then why don't you say so? Too coy?"

Ki snickered. She took him off guard. The only reason he hadn't given in to his passions was out of respect for her tragedy. The kinship he felt for her had been present from their first meeting.

She surprised him further by reaching back and lifting his hand from his thigh and placing it around her waist.

"Best hold on. Tight. No tellin' what a stallion's capable of."

Soon his hand was not just holding her, but rubbing her, and he could swear that her butt was swaying more than before. He pressed his face into her hair, and she turned to press her cheek against his. He placed his other hand on her waist and then raised it to her breast as he also reached down to her crotch. The horn obstructed his lower hand, but he gently cupped her breast with the other and flicked the hardening nipple through her shirt. She inhaled deeply and slid one hand behind her until she had Ki's rock-hard bulge in her palm. She squeezed and pressed it, rubbed it in every direction, while forcing herself more firmly against the horn. They both groaned with anxious lust, but, lowering her head, Arvilla removed her hand and slowly pushed Ki's away, fearing Jessie would turn. She turned her head sideways.

"I don't hold kindly to puttin' off pleasure. World's too damn crazy. This here's something I mean to see through, if you have a like mind, Ki, soon as this trouble blows over."

"I can't hardly wait, but you bet I will."

They kept to the high wilderness, expecting to crest the rim of Marmot Gulch sometime soon. Any higher and the stands of tall pine would thin out, making sightings too easy, so they meandered through rock-strewn forests for what seemed like an eternity. Upon reaching a wide, grassy alpine meadow, they paused, listening and watching, before moving slowly around the perimeter. Back among the trees, they heard a sound like wind blowing, but the treetops were still.

"Water," Ki said, and quietly dropped from the horse.

Within a few rods' distance, they saw the sparkle of a brook ahead and stood very still before approaching. On the far side was a rough wagon road that curved over the next hill. They gave it good long listen, then dismounted and watered themselves. Arvilla figured they should cross the road but avoid it otherwise. This was Gore territory.

Ki's ears pricked up, and in a desperate whisper, he warned, "Quick, get back! Wagons!"

As soon as they retreated into the brush, the drumbeat of hooves and the clatter of wagon wheels broke upon them. From over the hill rumbled a lorry laden with three dusty pine coffins and a teamster resting a scattergun in the crook of his arm. Although the road was poorly leveled and the leather leaf springs screeched and flexed, the long boxes bounced very little and rested heavily, making a deep knocking sound when they rocked side to side. Ki and the women held the animals' sights away from the commotion and stood vigilantly behind trees with guns ready. They watched as the two-mule team plodded up the next rise and the entire ponderous rig disappeared.

Again they waited.

When no other movement was heard, they dropped down to the road. Ki asked Arvilla what was on the other side of the hill where the wagon had come from. She shrugged.

"Nothin'. Far as I know, that road veers off thataways, away from the stream."

Suggesting they parallel the road until they could see a greater distance, Ki led them through the trees and up the hill. As he crested the rise and crept up for a view, the women kept the horses back. The road did, indeed, veer away from the stream, snaking into and out of the folds of the gullies, into and out of view. He listened carefully to the wind, and when it was safe, he signaled the others to follow.

But it wasn't safe. The wind shifted, and the sound of another wagon was upon it. A buckboard—this one carrying three miners—drawn by a single large mule, and an armed Blossom Rock Guardsman mounted on another rounded the nearest curve. There was no hiding. A miner in the buckboard spotted them through the trees.

Jessie and Arvilla cocked their weapons simultaneously upon hearing one of the men announce, "It's the ones that got away!" The Guardsman lifted his Spencer from its saddle holster, and the teamster drew a revolver. When the other miners realized they were in line to catch stray lead, they hopped off the far side of the wagon and scrambled for cover, but the volley was brief.

A crack shot, Arvilla drew a bead, and her first round slammed into the stock of the Spencer, damaging the magazine within and knocking the rifle out of the Guardsman's hand just as the barrel cleared leather. Seeing the determined young markswoman lever the Winchester as she advanced, the Guardsman dug his heels hard into the beast and made a run for it, yelling for his friends in the wagon far ahead, out of hearing range. Arvilla swept herself into her saddle and bolted after him. She caught up to the surefooted mule in moments. Coming alongside the Guardsman and grasping the Winchester by the barrel, she swung it like a club, yelling with the exertion. The buttstock met the back of his skull with a solid crack but didn't drop him, so Arvilla lifted the weapon again, bringing it down with all her might for a rib-crushing blow to his back. The Guardsman tumbled beneath the flailing hooves of his mount, almost causing Arvilla's to stumble. She spurred the stallion harder, took the rifle in her other hand, and reached for the frenzied mule's rein. Looping it fast around the horn of her saddle, she pulled the stallion back with gritted teeth and brought the mule to an abrupt stop.

While she was on the run, Jessie and Ki moved apart to confuse the teamster, whose first shot was directed at Jessie. Dropping to one knee and turning sideways, Jessie presented a small target and heard the *zing* of the bullet in front of her face. Fanning off two rounds, she hit the teamster once in the shoulder and he ducked, shooting, into the wagon.

"I don't want to kill you!" Jessie shouted. "But I will if you don't drop the gun!"

The teamster rose up on one hand, yelling, "Kiss my ass!" and took aim, but Ki had already drawn back the hammer of his Russian revolver and smashed the teamster's wrist with one well placed shot. The pistol fell to the ground and discharged, wounding the sumpter in the flank. The enraged animal thrashed and kicked, then ran off the side of the road and, before falling to its knees, toppled the careening wagon onto the screaming teamster. The remaining muckers turned tail and raced for denser wood. Jessie put down the wounded mule mercifully, and they hurried on their way before the echoes of their gunplay returned with curious Gore men.

By noon, the three of them stood looking down upon the switchbacks and headframes, the mine-car rails and stamp mills of the Gore Company, high above Redemption. The somber sky began to release a tearful rain, and deep growls of thunder followed a faint shimmer of lightning. Here beneath a copse of lodgepole pines, the three riders waited for nightfall before descending into that earthly hell.

Just as the advancing mountain shadows fell across the town, Ki made a surprising sighting. Calling the women's attention, he pointed out a lumbering wagonload of coffins they had seen hours earlier. The teamster drew up to the Keepsake adit and backed the lorry to it. Four men came down from the shaft house and loaded the coffins atop hand-trammed mine cars. The work was obviously difficult as the boxes were slid across planks and not lifted. They definitely were not empty.

★

Chapter 13

Klue, the Gore assayer, awoke with his head ringing to find himself tied and gagged beneath a table in his own office. Before him, he could see only the legs of the man responsible, but couldn't recognize him by his boots, except that he was tall. The jackleg owlhoot who'd clobbered him from behind was throwing on some baggy miner's denims and a thigh-length coat that Klue kept in the back. The intruder whistled as he gathered odds and ends into his saddlebag. Finally he left, flipping over the sign in the window to read "Closed" and snapping shut the hasp of a heavy lock through the door latch. Pulling Klue's floppy felt hat over his brow, the stranger turned into the street, removed a key from a large ring of keys, and pocketed the rest. Turning off Eagle Road, he chucked the key into the brush and headed uphill. Coleson didn't want anyone untying Klue before the ornery assayer had worked himself up into a real good lather.

Marmot Gulch's typically early sundown was accompanied by a downpour. The switchbacks rising to the mine entrances were awash. Coleson trudged through the gullywasher higher and higher, exhausted at that elevation.

He headed for a small shack built into the ground by itself at trail's end, but paused. Two men were waiting out the rain beneath the shack's awning. He opened his coat and tucked one side behind his holster, exposing the grip of his Colt. He circled up behind the building and crept slowly around.

At the building's edge, he shouted, "Hey!" The miners turned with a start, and Coleson swung a two-pound sledge, bringing it savagely across the nearest man's jawbone. The second miner reached inside his coat for something, but Coleson was faster. He whipped out the double-action Army and drilled two slugs through the miner's sternum. The man fell sideways into the mud and looked about to yell for help, but Coleson cut him off with a hard-swung boot to the face that turned him belly-up for the rain to thin his gushing blood.

A sign on the locked door read, "DANGER—EXPLOSIVES. DO NOT ENTER."

The echoing gunshots were like a bugle call to everyone who expected trouble—including Jessie, Ki, and Arvilla, who were already descending into the valley, racing toward the Keepsake. They knew Coleson would be the most likely person on one end of that weapon, hopefully not the business end. But several others on the barren slopes were also alerted—Ryde Benton among them.

Coleson couldn't find the key to open the lock. He dropped the ring and bashed the lock with the blood-daubed sledge until the entire latch fell away. A minute later he reemerged from the shack, his saddlebag heavy with stolen explosives and a huge coil of safety fuse slung over his shoulder. Like a deer, he sprang from the shack and headed for the hulking stamp mill downhill from the Keepsake headframe.

The mill, situated lower on the slope than the mines that fed it, stood at the end of a curving, elevated railway from which mine cars dropped ore into the hoppers. As Coleson came beneath the railway bridge, the four men who were in the Keepsake shaft house appeared, coming

162

toward him, having heard the shots. He hid in the shadows beside a timber piling and was startled by someone hissing close by.

"Psst! Coleson! Stay put. They ain't seen ya."

It was Nettles. He had been watching Coleson, hardly believing what he saw. The old marshal walked into the miners' path, staggering. His Peacemaker was in his hand.

"Hey!" he shouted at them, "which one o' you boys gonna fetch me a spade? I got some gold to dig in that thar hole. Whar's the shovels?"

Three of the men were Blossom Rock Guards. The fourth was Kyle, the scrawny shift boss. The hand Coleson had shattered in the livery stable was hidden beneath his oilcloth slicker. He was the only one among them wearing one. They were exasperated upon seeing the old lawman.

Kyle shouted, "What in blazes you doin' up here, Kentucky? Who you shooting at?" Another taunted, "You blessed crazy, you mangy ol' sheep? Huh? You loco?"

Nettles pulled a flask from his pocket and threw back a swig. Wiping his mouth with his sleeve, he barked, "Whar's the gol'dang spades, you varmints? I wanna spade!"

With that, he cocked the Peacemaker. Teetering on his feet, he waved it and threatened the skittish men to a standoff, then fell to his knees and pulled the trigger, which resulted in an anticlimactic *click*.

"Hey, Kentucky," Kyle said with a sigh, "you'd be considerable more afright'nin' if'n you'd load your gun." Together they turned back toward the shaft house, never laying eyes on Coleson. One of them called back, "It's comin' down a deluge, you old sumbitch! Git home and sleep it off! . . . And don't fire that gun again!"

When they were out of sight, Nettles stood and stomped off the mud and gravel. He looked back at Coleson and nodded, reloaded the empty chamber, and continued uphill with a steady gait.

Although the massive stamping machinery inside the mill stood idle, the four great furnaces were under steam.

Coleson cautiously peeked through the door and entered. Before him stood two dozen ore bins in a row, above them the monstrous array of solid steel stamps rising vertically eighteen feet in the colossal timber frame. Each of the two sets of stamps rode upon a steel camshaft attached at one end to an iron flywheel nearly twelve feet in diameter. Small by industry standards, the mill was nonetheless integral to the Gore Company's ore processing.

Where the nearest stamp frame stood upon its gigantic bed plate, Coleson placed a small bundle of dynamite and quickly rigged the blasting caps. He ran a length of fuse to a window and tied off another length to the second frame, where he duplicated the sabotage. Having united the fuses into one closely timed coil, he smashed out the window and fed everything through. Hopping out after them, he ran the line a hundred yards to a short train of ore cars standing on the rails to the Keepsake.

He fed the jute-wrapped fuse through the spoked wheel of an ore car and tied it to the opposite wheel so that the fuse was horizontal and taut, an inch above the axle and out of the rain. With a knife, he cut a short piece and tied a three-inch candle he had stolen from the assay office to the top of the axle, beneath and at a right angle to the fuse. He rooted through his bag and found matches, but repeated striking wouldn't light the water-soaked sulphur. He cursed and dug through his bag frantically.

Ryde Benton rode a panting mule up the switchbacks and was soon abreast of the explosives cache. He hopped to the ground, letting the animal wander, and squinted his colorless eyes in the driving rain. Thunder rolled off the hogbacks like an avalanche. He was about to walk ahead toward the stamp mill when lightning turned the mountainside to daylight. In the dancing blue-whiteness he saw the two bloodied miners, one of them sitting up against the wall with half his face torn open almost as wide as the door of the shack. When he discovered Coleson's theft, he ran out, hurling curses.

Beneath the ore car, Coleson carefully pried open a small detonator cap, fearing it would flash in his face. He tapped a small bit of mercuric fulminate into a cone of paper torn from one of his guidebooks. He inserted a small piece of the gunpowder-filled fuse for good measure. Folding the paper closed, he placed it on a flat rock held in his palm and, averting his face, slapped it with a rock in his other hand. The fulminating powder blazed, igniting the fuse and the paper and allowing him to light the candle wick. He figured he had eight to ten minutes before the shrinking candle drew its flame to the fuse above. Gathering his bag, he bolted for the Keepsake.

That's when Benton spotted him in a day-bright shudder of lightning, sprinting toward the mine.

Nettles was still ascending the small-gauge rails when he saw Coleson sidestep the ore car standing at the portal of the Keepsake and vanish inside. Blinking hard, he saw Benton in fast pursuit and raised his Peacemaker with both hands.

"Benton! Stop where y'are! It's the law! Stop or I'll shoot!"

Three reverberating blasts shook the hillside. Jessie, Ki, and Arvilla drove their mounts on a hock-skinning downhill plummet. Ki was the first to make it to the mine-car rail, where he saw Coleson and Benton disappear into the mine's blackness. He leapt from his saddle while still in motion and bolted after them. Shots rang out from above, kicking up mud just inches away from his feet. They were answered by gunfire from below as Nettles tried to hold off the fast-approaching Guardsmen from a dangerously unprotected position.

Seeing Nettles in the open, Jessie and Arvilla put up a withering crossfire. Firing low off the shoulder at full gallop, Arvilla shattered the thighbone of one Guardsman and made the others scatter, while Jessie took a stand beneath a shelf of rock projecting over the Keepsake entrance. No one could fire down on her, and the empty ore car at the portal became her bunker. In moments, Arvilla and the panting marshal joined her.

"Help me pull it over," Jessie shouted, and together they held to one side of the car and, using all their weight, rocked it onto its side. No sooner had it fallen than Kyle was firing at them using his good, but less accurate, hand. Deadly ricochets *spanged* off the rock wall behind them, and the timber shoring splintered and cracked. Arvilla's superior skill soon pinned the three shooters to the wet ground. A worried look overcame Nettles while he reloaded.

"Uh-oh. Here come their girlfriends," he said.

Coming up the dark switchbacks was a procession of bobbing lanterns.

Thinking fast upon entering the mine, Coleson snatched up an oil lantern as he hopped over railway ties and abandoned tools. He ran until he couldn't see anything, then walked with one hand on the wall. The sounds of dripping water and scampering rodents made him strain to see through the inky blackness. He stumbled and caught himself. Feeling a deep niche in the wall, he pressed himself into it and used fulminating powder from the opened blasting cap to get a lamp lit. Now running at almost full speed, he receded far enough into the tunnel to prevent Benton from benefiting from the light.

But Benton had been through these tunnels hundreds of times and knew them better than he knew most places aboveground. He walked confidently, steadily watching for his chance . . . all the while unaware that Ki had followed them.

In the wide stope, Coleson set the lamp beside a wall near the entrance. A mine car within cast a shadow over the back wall. In the convection from the shaft, a large ventilating fan lazily spun. He dropped his saddlebag and removed the explosives, leaving some extra blasting caps inside. Suddenly he felt the ground tremble and heard a deep rumble. He had grossly overestimated when the stamp mill would blow.

166

Having quickly inspected the shafts and machinery, he climbed into the ore hoist. There was a gap between the shaft wall and its timber shoring, so he planted a few sticks of dynamite inside it, secured them with chips of stone, and ran the fuse out toward the steam engine. Several more sticks were crammed into crevices beneath the machinery and fuses attached. Hastily he ignited the mercuric fulminate, so desperate now his hands shook.

Coming into the light, Benton's eyes were pained. He expected an ambush until he saw Coleson recklessly squatting over the machinery with his back to the entrance.

As Coleson touched the fire to the fuse, the crunch of gravel made the hair on the back of his neck stand up. He leapt over the hoisting drum just as Benton whirled a rusted pickax end over end, sending up sparks against the machinery where Coleson had stood.

The geologist drew his Colt Army and fired, the blast magnified to deafening proportions in the rocky confines. But Benton had already retreated to the darkness and continued to hurl anything he could lift, whether stone or tool. Coleson fired nervously, knowing his chances for getting out alive had just been cut in half.

The impossibly loud bursts of gunfire made Ki's ears ring. He inhaled deeply to relax as he went, adept in the "little steps" of *ko-ashi*, the art of careful walking. At one point he struck something heavy—an ore car on the rails. Making terribly slow progress in the darkness, he stayed close to the wall, getting fleeting glimpses of the mine's contours with every lightning flash from outside and, later, with every gun blast from within.

The first time his hand fell across a piece of metal jutting out from the wall, he avoided it. Then it dawned on him. Candle-holders pinned into the rock. He moved forward about five feet and ran his hands across rough-cut timber and jagged stone until he found another one. It was covered with melted wax, but held no candle. Again he moved forward, and finding a candle in the next holder, he produced a match and lit it. Cupping his hand around the weak flame, he sped deeper into the mountain.

Coleson raked the width of the tunnel with nerve-shattering blasts until he had spent his rounds. While exchanging the Colt for his .44–40, Benton let out a bloodcurdling holler and heaved a rock the size of his own head. Coleson slapped his hand across the Merwin's hammer and fired recklessly while ducking the stone.

The light blinked out with a thundering echo and the tinkle of broken glass, and they were plunged into total darkness but for the pale, sputtering flame of the burning fuse.

"Now what you gonna do, mama's boy?" taunted Benton from the shadows. "You don't know this hole like me. You're like to stumble in one of them four-hunnerd-foot pits you standin' by. Nobody'd even hear you scream."

Benton moved along the wall, staying low behind the ore car, until he came to a dark niche. There he stood stock still and silent. He could hear Coleson's nervous breathing. Benton quietly squatted and lifted a small stone. He threw it across the stope and shut his eyes.

Coleson's gun boomed, vomiting fire that momentarily blinded him.

Benton flung another stone elsewhere, and Coleson's next shot followed it. Benton lifted a large rock. He stood and heaved it straight for the exhausted geologist, shattering his forearm and triggering a discharge. He lost the weapon as his head slammed hard against a wall. Benton lifted another rock and, stepping over Coleson's saddlebag, moved in.

The fuse fire fluttered in the breezes they caused, and shadows danced crazily across the irregular walls. Coleson sat up and tried to focus his eyes as Benton's shadowy bulk came on. The ventilating fan's blades were spinning faster, throwing flickering shadows across Coleson's drawn face. The fallen saboteur took his gun in his good hand, fired. Missed.

168

"Your last better be your best," Benton warned in his deep, airy voice.

Coleson's pistol practically hung from his weakened hand. After a moment, Benton stood closer, to find Coleson's eyes half-closed, his hands and feet trembling. He called to him, but Coleson didn't respond. In the grip of a seizure, the hapless saboteur dribbled.

Stuffing Coleson's gun into his belt, Benton lifted him bodily and dumped him into the ore car.

"You gonna take a little ride an' visit an old friend of mine," Benton grunted. He got behind the car and pushed.

Following the rails out of the eerie stope, Benton handtrammed the car faster with every step. It took a sudden veer to one side, heading down the slanting drift of the forgotten Sightless pillar mine, crushing the "Do Not Enter" sign to slivers. With a strained yawp, the big man released the car and listened to it rumble down the track. It crashed with a strident screech and clang against the pile of refuse at the bitter end and violently overturned, dumping Coleson beside the putrid remains of Orrum Jessup and pinning his leg fast to the jagged rock below.

"Coleson! John Coleson!" came Ki's voice from the far-off darkness.

The hulking mine superintendent drew Coleson's Merwin Hulbert and walked back toward the stope. The sound of its hammer being drawn back alerted Ki far in advance. He set down the candle. When Benton inched into the faint firelight, Ki was standing behind the wall watching the little fire crawl along the fuse, now only feet from its final destination.

The gun entered the stope first. Ki's vise grip locked onto Benton's wrist, and he pushed it high. With a chilling spirit yell, he pummeled the big man's abdomen with a pile-driving forward punch. Benton's face dropped to meet Ki's jaw-crushing hand-heel strike with the sound of shattering teeth.

169

Only stunned, Benton wound up and thrust his anvil right fist mightily upward into Ki's stomach. Nearly lifted off his feet, Ki doubled over and lost his breath, grasping at Benton's shirt to break his fall. In doing so, he tore away the canvas pouch that hung by a cord from Benton's neck. He saw the next deadly blow coming. He turned and caught Benton's fist in mid-flight. In continuous motion, he pulled the big man forward, using his own momentum to throw him off balance, whereupon he thrust a knee deep into Benton's liver and delivered a devastating kidney punch with his middle knuckle extended.

Ki found the gutta-percha grips of the Russian in his belt and pulled it as Benton fell.

"Don't make me shoot, Benton. This mine's gonna blow, and I'm taking you outta here alive."

"The hell you are," Benton growled from the floor. He slung a handful of gravel into Ki's face. The gun went off uselessly, and Benton sideswiped his blinded foe with a rock-hard fist. From his wet, muddied jacket, he pulled out the bone-handled blade that had been Orrum Jessup's demise and pounced.

Ki's acute gut sense felt him coming, and he rolled smoothly to the floor. Through his watery eyes he saw the handle of the pickax and grabbed it. Benton went for Ki's shirt with the fluted, blued-steel blade cocked back like the head of a riled rattlesnake. Holding the pick handle at either end Ki deflected his arm, then thrust the iron head upward to connect with the side of Benton's bovine head, which got bashed again when he landed backward upon the rail behind him.

Reaching out to his side, Benton found Coleson's saddlebag. Rolling to his feet, he swung it at Ki, who avoided it easily. Benton swung again. The bag struck a vertical shaft timber and burst into a raging fireball, detonated by the blasting caps within. The explosion maimed both of Benton's forearms and scorched his bleeding head as it threw him backward to the yawning mouth of the shaft. With eyes wide and wild with terror, he teetered on the precipice unable to regain his balance, snatching a last, frozen glance at his stunned opponent, and with a bellowing shriek he arced back into the plutonian void, falling and falling the four hundred feet to a softly splashing finale.

Darting down the Sightless drift as fast as the candle flame allowed, Ki reached Coleson. He knelt down to rouse him, gasping when the eroded profile of the unfortunate Jessup became visible. He tried lifting Coleson before realizing his leg was pinned. His first efforts to move the mine car failed, so he put his back against it, and with his feet against the solid wall, he pushed and lifted it enough to pull Coleson's leg out.

The bruised and battered man mumbled and groaned. He fought to lift his eyelids, and when he succeeded, he leapt with a wakeful yelp at the sight of his deceased companion lying beside him. Noticing that the corpse's right arm ended abruptly in shattered bone, he recalled Jessie's account of the grisly parcel sent through the window at Atwood's ranch. He looked more closely. In the V of Jessup's collar, he noticed a thin cord around his neck. He tugged at it until he could see the object hanging from it, a small brass locket. With a snap, Coleson broke it away and cried, "Get me the hell outta here! This whole place is gonna blow!"

Turning him over his shoulders, Ki carried him up the midnight tunnel, scrambling to keep his footing on the railway ties and debris. The candle threatened to blink out at every step. As they hurried through the stope, Ki saw the small pouch he had torn from Benton's neck and stooped to retrieve it. Coleson, seeing the fuse barely more than an inch long, yammered in fear. Ki raced out, assuring him they'd make it.

"Ain't no way we're gonna make it! Ain't no way!" Coleson yelled, his voice becoming shrill. "Goddamn it, Ki, put me down and run! We'll never make it!"

Close enough to the adit to see Jessie behind the overturned mine car, Ki noticed the ore car he had stumbled against on the way in.

"I'm dropping you, but we're both getting outta here," he said.

He put Coleson down and, with Herculean effort, managed to turn the ore car onto its side. Getting behind it, he pushed hard and inverted it atop a large rock that kept it off the ground on one side.

"Get under!"

Once they had shimmied underneath, Ki instructed, "Push out the rock when I lift and stay clear."

He put his back to the inside top of the car and pressed upward while Coleson struggled against the stone. Ki strained to maintain a constant lift, but the massive car fell against the odd-shaped rock again and again. Each time, he grunted like an overburdened ox.

"I can't move it!" cried Coleson. "Lift! Higher!"

The earth beneath them shuddered. A breathtaking orange flash illuminated the tunnel in a hellish light never witnessed by the living. With his face near the ground, Coleson saw the monstrous, roiling conflagration billowing toward them through the rectangular tube, roaring with a violence and wrath of Biblical dimensions. He felt the air move across his face, and barely a heartbeat before the hellfire could incinerate them, the ore car lifted, the stone pushed free, and blessed blackness surrounded them.

The scalding concussion pounded the mine car several inches forward, throwing Ki atop his injured companion. The stupendous roar of ruptured bedrock blended with an infernal chorus of screaming timbers shattering under pressure, rushing hot gases howling like banshees, and vulture wings of fire fluttering overhead.

And still the resonant booming continued. Timbers just outside their iron cocoon shivered and were torn from the ground in which they stood. The deafening pounding of tons of raw stone upon the car could barely be drowned out by

172

the two men's incessant screaming—voices impossible to hear outside.

But Jessie, Nettles, and Arvilla did hear the hollow-sounding rupture within the Keepsake. They felt the very mountain beneath them convulse. They had not had reason to fire their guns again since the procession of lantern bearers showed themselves to be a cadre of soldiers out of Fort Steele, hurriedly dispatched by order of Jessie's friend, Colonel Bobbitt. But now, under a choking black cloud of rock dust and smoke, they fell away from the portal, Jessie having to be pulled by the arm by the old marshal to keep her at a safe distance from her companion's certain grave. A few moments passed. The rumbling ceased. The smoke settled.

Inside the Keepsake, under untold tons of earth lay the two men who recently had most closely touched Jessie's life.

★
Chapter 14

For the next five days, something overcame Redemption that hadn't been present in over seven years: silence. Smokestacks atop smelters stood clear of exhaust. Stamp mills and ore cars went idle. Steam engines lost pressure, and the hiss and squeal of hoists and pulleys gave way to the chirps of birds and the whisper of mountain winds.

There was little of the crude disorder that typified the mining camp, due mainly to the presence of the soldiers. The only places where silence met its match were in the saloons and brothels, where hordes of the Redeemed argued about the mayhem, about "them Texas muckrakers snooperin' about our business," about what fate was in store for them all. At the poker tables, accusations were now placed in favor of bets, but the tangle-foot flowed as usual. Suddenly there was talk of a new breed of Redeemed—the hero, usually self-appointed. They bragged about their feats accomplished during the three-day rescue of Ki and John Coleson from the very jaws of hell. The Redeemed who believed Jessie, Ki, and Coleson to be the true heroes were few in number and generally quiet.

The two survivors of the Keepsake blast had been pulled out from under their iron shield after rescuers could no longer doubt the voices and pounding they had thought were imagined. Many of them even feared the survivors. It was impossible, they said, to be underground that long without air—fire gobbles it all up. They must be demons. Even the stubbly-faced horse doctor who patched Coleson up claimed, "They scare me pea-green." All Ki needed was a good rest and a few hot meals. It all seemed too strange. It occurred to Coleson that some lucky jackleg would be selling tickets to visitors wanting to see where the "Redemption demons walked the earth."

Even more, he wondered how soon he could see his low-down, snake-bellied stepfather hanged for murder.

As he convalesced in a room above the St. Ives Saloon, Coleson learned from Jessie and Ki of the progress of the inquest being conducted by the young Army officer in charge. He was miffed that Padgett, a pillar of the community, was not in jail, but had simply been ordered not to skip town.

The evidence of Padgett's responsibility for all that was wrong about Redemption seemed overwhelming; yet proof of conspiracy to murder eluded the authorities. Coleson himself was little help during the first two days after his rescue. His leg and arm were so bad off, he floated on a cloud of laudanum when he wasn't eating. The initial visits he received from Jessie, Ki, Arvilla, and the young officer he could not later recall. The officer posted day and night guards to prevent retaliation, a favored sport in Redemption, and no one passed into that room without permission.

Except Padgett.

In the dead of night, Coleson dreamed that his door squeaked and a diminutive dark figure entered. He was fighting to wake up from the foreboding nightmare when he recognized the thin mustache and pale skin and realized it was no dream.

Shaking the opium cloud somewhat, Coleson tried to raise his head and mumbled, "How'd you get in?"

Padgett smiled and shook his head. He spoke in a whisper. "Don't you know me well enough by now to realize that Army regulars pose the least threat of all? They're more easily bought than the burrowing muckworms that infest towns like this."

He stood at the foot of the bed, eyeing the blood-soaked, bandaged arm that rested over the clean white bed sheet covering Coleson. The injured leg was elevated, the foot exposed. Coleson's eyes blinked, unable to focus.

"So you finally found me, ay, boy? What did you think you could do? Put me in jail? Kill me?" He exhaled with a smirk and touched Coleson's toe. "I am this town. I decide what happens here. I pull the levers."

He gave the toe an abrupt yank, twisting it hard. Coleson sputtered in pain that cut through his opium fog. His heart raced, giving him greater clarity and focus.

"If you thought for a minute that I'd give you the slightest opportunity to avenge your mother, then you're denser than even I suspected." He twisted the blue-black toe once more, eliciting a crackling groan from the stricken man. "And you're stupider still for thinking I'd let you live after all the trouble you've caused."

Padgett walked to the side of the bed and leaned over slightly. His eyes bored into Coleson's.

"I thought I would strangle you myself, just for the extreme pleasure of it. But then . . . How are your seizures lately, boy? I understand that swallowing one's tongue during seizures is a real danger. Could cause suffocation." Withdrawing an apothecary vial from his jacket pocket, he continued, "But then, so can this—in a manner of speaking. A bit messier perhaps."

He uncorked it.

"A favorite recipe of mine. Poison hemlock, milkweed, and vetch." From inside his jacket, he withdrew a smooth length of wood, the handle of a hammer. "Something to

176

remember your dear mother by."

He sprung, throwing one leg over the helpless man, and sat on his chest. Coleson bucked uselessly. His arms were pinned. Capping the vial with his thumb, Padgett forced the handle between Coleson's lips with both hands, leaning with all his might. He worked to wrench Coleson's teeth open. Coleson weakly shook his head, tried to yell without opening his mouth, but Padgett was in full control.

Coleson snorted. His teeth separated, and the handle pried open his jaw like a port bit, stretching his flesh painfully. He saw the vial begin to pour its weed-smelling fluid, felt the first cold splash on his lip. The sheet above his good hand tented up beneath Padgett. Two back-to-back bursts of gunfire ripped into Padgett's abdomen through the anus. The murderer fell upon Coleson, then toppled to the floor. Writhing in agony, his pants staining with blood, Padgett looked up in disbelief. Coleson lifted his shrouded double-action Colt and drilled a burning chunk of lead into Padgett's forehead and out the back, spattering the wall beyond with a shower of blood, hair, and bone.

When the Cornish couple who owned the St. Ives burst in, Padgett lay on his back, clutching the vial tightly in his fist.

In the days following, the inquest resulted in formal charges against Kyle and several Blossom Rock Guardsmen, and a complete report was made on the massacre and the mine blasts. The enormity of the crimes exceeded the young officer's experience and made upstanding people throughout the region reel with disgust.

Understanding Benton's derangements was just a matter of viewing the four-fingered hand he had delivered to Arvilla, or inspecting the content of his little canvas pouch—the desiccated nose of a Cheyenne murdered and mutilated by him at Sand Creek. His alliance with Padgett had less to do with greed than with his own blood-simple lunacy and limitless hatred.

177

Coleson himself proved that most of Padgett's assays had been falsified. The samples of Never Sleep ore he had smuggled out bore little likeness to what Padgett's own assays claimed, as the report he hid in the barrel of Nettles's Remington-Rider proved. After all, it was prepared by a Starbuck assayer in Denver. The carbon copies he'd stolen from Klue's waste pail corroborated everything.

As Coleson said during a session of the inquest conducted at his bedside, "I had to prove that Padgett was salting his mines. That way he inflates stock value, unloads the claims without loss. There's the proof. Starbuck assays are the best. Ain't no need to dig out them coffins full of high grade."

Afterward, everyone filed out, but Coleson called Jessie back. He held her hand a long while in silence. He called her "remarkable."

"I'm fairly impressed by you, too, John Coleson," she said, sitting beside him. "But I'm still not convinced that's your real name."

He laughed.

"No, it's my real name. Sometimes I wish it weren't." He suddenly looked serious. "Yesterday that Army fella said they might charge me with arson."

It wasn't a complete surprise to her. She said, "The Keepsake was worthless anyhow, and with all the people—"

Coleson cut her off. "Not for the Keepsake. The Never Sleep," leaving Jessie at a loss for words. "Yep. That Army fella thinks that evidence the Gore Company conjured up points to me."

"Well, does it?"

Coleson pursed his lips and nodded.

"Doubt they could prove anything. But that ain't why I asked you back. Two things: First, I'd like you to telegraph a friend of mine in Denver, an old Wells Fargo buddy. Second, I was hoping we could get together again. The way we did at Gracious Creek. Sure was something to recollect."

"You must be feeling healthy again," she replied. Drawing her hand across a certain bulge in the blanket, she said,

"Oh, my! You are feeling better!"

Gathering the blanket around his sturdy erection, Jessie stroked him and bent to kiss him. Brazenly she drew down the sheet and lifted his nightshirt. She held his rigid cock straight up, squeezing it firmly, and said, "Hmm, pretty soon you'll be standing up as well as this one is." She went down on him voraciously, the heat of her mouth sending fire into his loins. She stroked his shaft in rhythm to the rising and falling of her head and hummed with pleasure as his body went stiff. He jetted streams of cum into her hungry throat while she milked every last drop and licked him clean.

Drawing back the covers and kissing him on the lips, she said, "Now get some rest so you'll be strong enough to go from there."

In moments, he was blissfully unconscious.

Rejoining Ki outside, Jessie suggested they take a meal at the Touchstone. Ki was startled to see the blond tresses of Lydia Boudreaux bouncing toward them. She was dressed in a handsome burgundy outfit that was modest by her standards. She carried luggage. Walking up to Ki, she put down her bags and, reaching into her bodice, produced a folded sheet of paper.

"I think you should have these," she said, handing them to Ki. "They are genuine Gore assays. The *real* assays, not the ones Klue does. I took them from Padgett's safe." Jessie asked her why she was doing this, and she looked at Ki. "It's something I should have done a long time ago."

"What are you going to do now?" asked Ki.

Picking up her bags, she said, "I'm leaving Redemption. For good."

Ki realized there was a coach just arriving down the road.

Lydia continued, "Gonna try my luck in Steamboat. If that don't work, there's plenty more towns to find work. Or a husband."

Two days later, on her routine morning visit to Coleson, Jessie found his room empty, the bed disheveled. On the pillow was a copy of his *Guide to the Mineral Treasures of the Great Basin* with a message scrawled across the cover:

Dear Jess,
 Apologies for sudden departure. Army wants me to redeem myself. Will be healthier than ever when I come to Texas to write new guide to oil fields. See you there.
Love, J.C.

Coleson's departure was a complete surprise to the Cornish proprietors. They said Coleson had had another visitor just the night before, said he was with Wells Fargo. Coleson, always the gentleman, had left payment for their services beneath his pillow.

Traveling bag in hand, Jessie stood before a stagecoach near the newspaper building on Eagle Road. High on the ridge, the collapsed walls and timbers of the stamp mill now lay piled within the charred remains of its exterior frame. Ki removed his satchel from Atwood's buckboard while Arvilla Jessup stayed close, not wanting to say good-bye, not knowing how. Ki set down his bag and gave Arvilla a gentle hug, saying words Jessie didn't hear, then handed the baggage up to the driver.

"What's going to happen to all this?" Arvilla asked, indicating the Gore Company's expansive operations.

"Probably be sold off to some conglomerate or parceled off. Someone honest, I hope. Arvilla, you should come to the Circle Star and stay with us awhile," Jessie offered.

Arvilla thanked her but declined.

"I got a heap of work to keep me busy here," she said. "Judge Atwood left a will in safekeeping. He and my father were close, you know. So . . . you're looking at the new owner of the Grand River Mining and Milling Company!"

With the Talisman being one of the last great lodes to be found north of the San Juans, Jessie thought it was only fitting. Arvilla's plans to build another home on Gracious

180

Creek met with her strong approval and made it easier to leave without her feisty old friend.

As the coach jostled downhill, Jessie and Ki were somber. Many of the Redeemed stood watching them go by. The Gore Assay Office came into view, its doors locked shut. Ki removed something from his vest and leaned out the open window. He jerked his arm, catapulting a metallic blur that made impact in the very center of the office door. Bearing the circle-S brand, the yin-yang symbol of the Starbuck empire, the throwing star was for all to see— the calling card of the Lone Star duo.

From the Creators of Longarm!

Featuring the beautiful Jessica Starbuck and her loyal half-American half-Japanese martial arts sidekick Ki.